Sain[illegible] Jawbone

By

Fiona Law

To my dear friends,
Grace & Grant; a jolly
little tale to enjoy.
Love Fiona Law

Eternal Press
A division of Damnation Books, LLC.
P.O. Box 3931
Santa Rosa, CA 95402-9998
www.eternalpress.biz

Saint Alba's Jawbone
by Fiona Law

Digital ISBN: 978-1-61572-226-6
Print ISBN: 978-1-61572-227-3

Cover art by: Amanda Kelsey
Edited by: Stephanie Parent
Copyedited by: Sherri Good

Printed in the United States of America

I'd like to dedicate this to my mother, Rose, with all my love.

Godwick is a lost town in Norfolk, England. It began as a village in the early-to-middle Saxon period but in the 1500's it began to decline (everyone up and left) until it disappeared due to - among other factors - climate change. Saint Alba and Saint Toole never existed - I made them and their stories up.

Chapter One

Winchester, England 1363

There was no harm in looking, in being tempted, Clara Baxter decided, so she sent her maid on ahead.

"Go now; you're needed in the kitchen at this hour," she said, and took the long way home unescorted.

Her skin still tingled from her visit to the stews. One of life's luxuries! One of the joys of being the daughter of a successful merchant in Winchester. It was a good life.

"*Gardey loo!*" a cry warned from above.

She dodged into the middle of the cobbled street and, avoiding a pack donkey, caused a water carrier to spill some of his load. The burdened man staggered left then right, stepped in some horse dung, and muttered profanities. Clara winced. She glanced back apologetically and almost bumped into a pair of ragged girls begging from a gloomy alcove.

Leaving them behind, she hurried on, shunning the alleys and dingy side streets that led to the poorer laborer's houses—dark and narrow tunnels where the city echoed eerily.

As she approached the street with her favorite little shop, she promised herself sternly, "I shall *not* go in, merely pass it by..."

She tried to concentrate on the shop signs, swaying lazily above the wooden doors, set in crooked walls. The row of shoemakers advertised their trade with pictures of a shoe, the needle makers with a needle, and the glove makers' signs depicted a splendid pair of gloves.

The crowds, mostly making their way home, or hurrying through the cobbled streets to do some last bit of business, seemed to be pushing Clara over to the side closest to that special little shop, until the first leather merchant's sign creaked imploringly ahead of her.

"Upon reflection, I shall allow myself to peer in as I go by." That would do no harm, surely?

Her heart leapt to see that its shelf still leaned out onto the street; they were still open for business! She drew nearer and, looking down to be sure her pattens were firmly laced over her soft shoes, she lifted her skirts high and stepped over the vile gutter.

There it was, hanging temptingly just out of reach: the most exquisite belt ever to be fashioned in Winchester. It was made of leather, dyed to a rich shade of amber, and it boasted no less than twenty silver studs, each etched with lines that radiated out from the center—twenty brilliant, miniature suns. And in the center of each, a polished garnet stone glistened. The belt was extravagantly long and was a little thicker than fashion prescribed, although it narrowed elegantly towards the end. An end that finished with a silver cap to match the buckle and the studs. *And* it came with an attached purse of the same warm yellow, in soft goatskin, and also with a silver clasp that hooked it firmly but elegantly to the belt. The purse possessed two long leather thongs, more for show than for function, as it had a buckle to close it properly. But at the ends of the thongs dangling down so temptingly were round garnet beads, knotted into place. And, as a final finishing, a thin sheath with matching beaded thongs, just the perfect size for a lady's knife, hung beside the purse.

Clara sighed rapturously. The leather merchant's wife, who knew the young visitor well, sighed too, but for a different reason. She unhooked the display and brought it closer, for Clara to see it better. Once again. Just in case...

"It pleases me to see that it's not yet sold," Clara said. Then, noticing the woman's frown, she added, "So that I may look at it. Selfish as that may be, I'm glad that I may behold it once more. 'Tis excellent work."

"You may touch it," the merchant's wife said after a pause, "if your hands are clean." Her own hands were spotless. And her face, peeking out of her tight gimp, had cheeks with the same ruddy shine of a polished apple.

Clara bent over the shelf, let her long fingers linger over the gems, and breathed out another sigh.

"I have, in my trunk, a russet kirtle, just the color of these garnets."

The merchant's wife smiled.

"I *do* believe, one day, I'll have cause to wear them together."

"You have a suitor?" she asked with interest. "Has your father found another...?"

"No. And, pray, don't say 'another' in such tones. You make it sound as though a thousand men have rejected me. And it was but one."

"You'll find someone one day. Have patience!"

"I do! Indeed, if it weren't for the prospect of wearing that lovely belt, I wouldn't care if I remained a spinster all the days of my life."

The merchant's wife drew a deep breath and gazed out into the street.

"I'm not a desperate woman," Clara frowned, "I merely want good reason to purchase that belt! I'm not...*am* I desperate?"

"Surely not! You adore the craftsmanship, as do I! Why not settle for this plain belt here? See, it is also of the same yellow leather." She pulled out another charming bit of leather work.

"Ah! That *is* lovely! But I have two similar belts from your shop."

"They make fine gifts."

Clara bit her lip. Her entire family—even their maid—all had little leather gifts from her. And all for the sake of that one piece, which drew her back to this shop week in and week out, like an enchantment. She had hoarded up enough money to buy it. Each visit to the stews, she put the correct sum to purchase it in her purse, then refused to buy it. Because good sense argued that she needed to have a reason to make such an expensive purchase. Such as the promise of a wedding day. But for that she needed to be engaged. Or did she? Perhaps, if she made this step first, put her faith in it, then the act of buying it would make it happen. The perfect man would step into her life, and all the rest would tumble effortlessly into place...

"Why did I not consider it thus, sooner," she murmured, and fixed her attention on the yellow leather belt studded with garnets, bending over it, tracing her fingers across it.

She didn't hear the door nearby slam, or see the young man stepping out into the street.

* * * *

He even glanced at the leather merchant's shop, but decided against browsing. There was time enough to shop later; he had a household to visit first.

Jack Paisley strode passed the leather merchant's shelf, grimacing as he braced himself against the concoction of smells that soiled the city air: stale urine, decaying flesh, rotting vegetables, raw sewage and, outrageously, he could detect the yeasty fragrance of warm bread drifting out from Baker's Street. As a child he'd taken deep breaths to get used to the odious mixtures quickly, and now he did the same.

Spotting a pie man, he adjusted his borrelais and crossed the crowded street. He didn't wish to drop in on his old master both unexpectedly and empty handed so near to dinner time. And a pie would be an excellent contribution. The hour of business was late, and he held a hand over the two remaining pies in order to detect some warmth.

"They're all freshly baked today, sir!" the seller assured him. As they spoke, and unbeknownst to them, Clara, eyes down as she pressed a little bundle tightly to her chest, passed them by.

Having made his purchase, Jack resumed his walk through the streets, using the cathedral tower as a beacon. He remembered the streets well, but the city had grown since he'd left it nearly seven years ago. He wondered that it had not burst out of its walls, it was so crowded with buildings, piling on top of one another, leaning askew over the cobbled streets. Dogs barked, hooves clopped, wheels ground on stone, doors banged shut and hinges creaked. He took it all in his stride, smiling a greeting here and there—and avoiding eye contact where necessary. A group of whores called out to him from an alley.

"Fancy a quick romp?"

"Ho, there, young cockerel, let me give you cause to crow."

"Come now, sweetheart, just a grout for some pleasuring!"

He ignored them all, unshaken, except when the last one called after him, "Would you take me for your *wife*? Do you not desire a buxom wife to cook and clean for you?"

His eyebrows flexed up and he glanced back quickly, stepping up his pace, putting distance between himself and the laughing whores. He smiled wryly. Poor wench had enough brain to be witty, and there she was—how had she had ended up in her position? Had she been born on the streets, or had she fallen from grace? Almost colliding with a stray pig, snapping and squealing as it fled by, brought him back to the matter at hand, and he concentrated on where he was going.

He walked with a jaunt, a fluid rolling from side to side as his long legs picked a path over the uneven streets. His fine, jaw-length curls bounced as he jumped to avoid rotting cabbage leaves, and other filth, in his way. How he loathed the city! Yet when he was traveling in the country, sleeping rough and enduring the continual damp and cold, he missed it.

Realizing that he'd passed his old master's house, Jack stopped and retraced his steps. He was aware of being watched by an armed soldier, although he pretended not to notice his audience. Soldiers sometimes sought after fights, and Jack always did his best to avoid combat. Like many tailors, Jack argued that he needed his hands and his eyes intact for the sake of his craft, but in truth, he was gentle by nature. Too calm and self-assured to be drawn easily into violent displays of manliness, he preferred to use his wit.

Recognizing his old master's house, Jack approached it purposefully before the soldier could find reason to hail him. It was small wonder he'd missed it. It had altered—grown—since he had left it. The scissors hanging above the door were new and larger too, and so was the emblem of the Tailors' Guild. The shelf opened out in front of the shop was being cleared by a familiar looking lad. Benedict, no doubt. His late mother's features were there in the boy right enough. Jack smiled at him, and he nodded back, but showed no sign of recognition. A young man Jack did not know was clearing the work bench behind the shelf, where the tailors could work in the full light of day. A journeyman, perhaps? And sweeping the floor was yet another apprentice!

And there was his old master, talking to a gentleman in a fur-trimmed coat, joined hose and mid-calf leather boots. A wealthy customer, no doubt. Jack hung about the entrance, watching young Benedict folding a piece of uncut flannel, until the customer left the shop with hearty laughter and enthusiastic handshaking. Then Jack peeked his head around the door and called, "Master Cedron Baxter, I'm glad to see that your business is thriving along with the city!"

Cedron took a moment to recognize his old apprentice before, with a delighted roar, he all but threw down the unfinished tunic in his hands and hastened to meet Jack. Cedron was not only wearing a tunic and joined hose of the finest materials, he had also grown a bit of a belly. His face had plumped out, and his jowls glowed with good health. The only thing that had thinned with time was his hair. He clapped Jack on his back so hard that he almost winded him.

"Ah, you still need to put a bit of flesh on those bones, eh? What brings you here, my lad? Are you looking for work? I now employ a journeyman and two apprentices—I'm sure you recognize Benedict, over there! But unfortunately, I don't really have place for another man just now."

"Nay, never!" Jack's square jaw jutted out, but his smiling gray eyes softened the look of pride. "I'm not seeking employment..."

"You're a master yourself? Do you need to rent a shop? Have you come home to join the Tailors' Guild?"

Jack scratched his ear. "Er...not exactly. I was merely passing through and—"

"You should settle down, lad! You're not afraid of producing your masterpiece, are you?"

"No, sir! I...er..."

"I taught you myself and can assure you that you're more than able..."

"Aye, I know." Jack threw his arm around Cedron's shoulder and directed their conversation away from the staring apprentices and journeyman. "I have a plan. I'm on my way to Bury. I liked it very well there, and I'm working my way back, to join the Bury Tailors' Guild."

He had a purse of coins tucked away, and some first-rate materials to sew his master piece from. But not here.

"What's so special about Bury? It boasts nothing that Winchester has not got."

"Aye, that is true. One city is much like the next, but...Bury speaks to me."

Cedron's eyes boggled. "*Speaks* to you?!"

"It's near where my grandfather hailed from...I know not how to speak it, sir. Winchester is special to me too, but I dearly wish to settle in Bury."

"Ah, well, at least I won't have to compete with your talent. Would you like to sup with us, before the curfew bell tolls?"

Jack nodded. "I have a pie," he said, and showed Cedron his contribution.

"Good! You can meet my new wife!" He beamed, leading Jack through the storeroom to the back of the shop. "See, I've added this space. I've bought the finest linens, and russets...and look at this frieze! And feel this heavy silk, from one of my ships."

Jack ran his long fingers down the cool satin of a gown draped on a table. The edgings were in the process of being embroidered with a floral trimming.

"That's the wedding gown for the mayor's daughter," Cedron said. "Our Clara is finishing it." With his hands on his hips, he gazed into the front of his shop. "Yes, I've had good luck in the last few years, son. See, I've dabbled a bit."

"Dabbled, sir?"

"In trade—nothing sinister," he hastened to explain, but if he had looked, he would have noticed the twinkle of amusement in Jack's eyes.

"Ah, trade! You had me troubled for a moment, sir."

"Trade is where the money is, Jack. I have good connections since I remarried. Indeed, that's how I met Juliet, my wife. I was purchasing silk from her father, when we found we enjoyed one another's company. Before I knew it I had put some money into one of his ships, and then some of the profits into another, and another. And somewhere along the way, I found myself married to Juliet."

Jack guessed that the marriage had taken place earlier on in the tale, rather than later, but he merely said, "I am very pleased for you, sir! Your happiness is well deserved!"

At that point, Cedron's eldest daughter interrupted their conversation as she entered the house through the back door. She had a little package in her hand. At the sight of her father, she quickly hid it behind her back.

Chapter Two

Clara hesitated for a moment, biting her bottom lip, but then shrugged and smiled.

"Father! What are you doing at the back of the shop? You ought to be out in the front, so that I might slip upstairs unnoticed. But here you are, loitering in the middle of my escape path. And with a customer to witness my crime. I may as well confess; I purchased an unnecessary and extravagant item with the whole of my allowance—my entire savings."

"Oh, be quiet, Clara!" Cedron snapped, then he said aside to Jack, "As you see, our Clara has not altered. Her tongue still wags faster than a puppy's tail!"

"Ah, but sir, she does not nag. A woman's wit is easier to endure than her nagging."

Cedron swiped at the air. "It's all torture to a man's ears: she should be bridled, I tell you, bridled! And Clara, this good man is a *guest,* not a customer. Do you not recognize our visitor?"

"A guest? Is this the hand of God at work? I buy an item fit to be a bridal gift and arrive home to find we have a gentleman guest? May I ask what is the purpose of this visit?"

Jack shifted slightly and stifled a cough.

"Stop your senseless wittering!" Conrad said. "Don't you see who this man is?"

Clara stared at Jack.

"My word," she said, "is it not Jack Paisley?!"

He bowed. "It is good to see you, Miss Clara."

"Has my apprentice not grown into a fine, upright freeman?" Cedron squared his shoulders. "Soon to be the member of a guild. Not that I'm trying to...ahem!"

Jack stifled another cough.

"I was...it was a private joke," Clara muttered.

"What a relief! You had me quaking in my boots."

She looked up from tweaking her kirtle and smiled. "You look well! Your hair's still...coppery. *Red* is such a fine, English coloring, Jack, would you not agree? I would have known you if I'd seen you in the street. Yes, I think I would have spotted you instantly."

She laughed lightly. "Aye, 'tis wonderful to meet you again. How are you?"

Jack held her gaze and rested a forefinger under his chin. "Very well, thank you, *Miss* Clara."

She blinked before drawing closer to him. "My, how astute of you! However, I have very high expectations with regards to marriage. Why, it could take years and years before we find a truly eligible *gentleman*. But, do tell, Journeyman Jack—my, how quaint that sounds, *journeyman*—pray, how have *you* fared over these past seven years?"

"Well, *Miss* Clara, *I* have reached *my* expectations."

"But as for mine; do I still *need* to find a husband?"

Cedron stepped between the couple. "Thank you, Clara, that will do. Quit your senseless banter! Pray, come Jack, come through to the solar!" Frowning at Clara, he ushered them upstairs.

While Cedron recounted all the additions and alterations he had made to the house, Jack quietly took in the upper room. The furnishings were more sumptuous than he remembered from previous years. Good pottery was set out on the strong table, the windows were paned with horn, and was that a decanter of wine? And goblets too! The tailor Cedron had done well since "dabbling in trade."

"My new mother's wedding gift," Clara said, tinkering with the goblets. One of them almost toppled over, but she caught it quickly and, glancing at her father, hastily began to pour out wine for all. Jack smiled as he thought how those fingers, which had embroidered such fine flowers earlier, were so clumsy now.

Noticing a red hue creep over her face, he tried to busy himself in listening to Cedron's conversation, which had now turned to his ventures in trade. Jack nodded and raised his eyebrows in the right places, but all the while, he found that his attention kept drifting toward Clara.

She had been a lanky girl, prone to tease and argue. It seemed she still enjoyed a good banter, but as many father figures like Cedron had warned him, a witty woman may charm a man into marriage; however, her sharp tongue would nag him to an early grave. And yet, she *was* beautiful. Her porcelain complexion showed off her dark almond eyes and high forehead. Her arched eyebrows and quick smile gave her face character, and her angular nose and square jaw gave it strength.

The two boys came up from the shop, scrubbed and combed. They kept quietly to themselves, muttering to one another in a corner. The odd bit of giggling and elbowing was as unruly as they got. Quieter still was the maid, who brought in the food and helped Clara serve. And her entrance was followed presently by a young woman. At first Jack though it must be Bridget or Gwendolyn—Clara's younger sisters—but Cedron took her hand and guided her forward.

"This is my wife, Juliet." He beamed.

Juliet was blonde and pretty, and comparatively very young. She wore a scoop-necked kirtle, not overly sumptuous but in a midnight blue, which enhanced the color of her eyes. Rather than the gimp to mark her married status, she wore her hair in an intricate plait, braided with satin ribbons and draped with a flimsy veil. A single pearl set with garnets in a striking design hung between her bare collarbones. Jack's eyes widened momentarily at the curve of her belly showing beneath the high waistline. He glanced at Clara, who was seated beside him. She met his eye and gave a tiny nod. Cedron fixed his focus on the far corner of the room.

Clara swallowed and said, "We are very fond of our new mother. Indeed, she was—is—a particular friend of my dear sister, Gwendolyn." She smiled amicably and took a sip of her wine. A lengthy sip.

Cedron nodded discreetly to her.

"Oh! And there's good news too," she added, "That is, *more* good news—the marriage is good news. I'm sure that Father and Juliet—*Mother*—will tell you themselves, in their own time, of course."

Juliet gave a little squeak and put her hands over her belly.

"Clara!" Cedron snapped. Then, puffing out, he turned to Jack. "As Clara has blurted out the news, I may as well tell you formally; we hope to have a child soon."

"I wish you all good health and great joy!" Jack beamed.

Clara leaned close to Jack as she passed a plate of lamb his way and whispered, "Father is proud and longs to tell everyone their good news, but Juliet is afraid of the birth. And so, having me tell the news, if anything goes wrong, *I'll* be to blame, *I* would have jinxed it."

The heady scent of garlic, rosemary and plump lamb curled its way through the room, and the red wine seemed to mellow the company's mood as the daylight began to fade. The wine and meat were plenty, and for a while Jack enjoyed hearing the news of the last seven years. Clara's youngest sister had died, but Gwendolyn was happily married to a butcher.

"Not long before Father and Juliet became engaged," Clara put in quietly.

"Clara! Hold your tongue!" Cedron shook his head and confided to Jack, "Hark how Clara babbles away like a rabid brook!"

"But she means no harm," Juliet said, "and at least her voice is gentle, even if it does go on."

"And on, and on! Alas! Methinks I'm destined to hear it all the days of my life!" Cedron glanced at Jack and looked down quickly.

"I'm sure she'll find a husband before long."

"Ha! But I hear no offers from you!"

"She's pretty, but..." Jack broke off and cleared his throat. Clara moved her board and knife an inch or two away from his.

"But will I ever get her off my hands!" Cedron took a gulp of his wine, "'Tis her mouth—the constant nattering. Such outspokenness in a woman is most unbecoming—it drives the men away. Small wonder her betrothal was cancelled."

Jack could almost feel the heat from the deep blush that spread over Clara's face.

"Nay, it was because he found me too tall, not because I speak too readily. Do you remember I was betrothed to Richard de Gaul?"

"I never liked him much," Jack replied.

"I grew head and shoulders taller than him, and he said it would cost too much to dress a woman of such a high stature."

"You are well rid of him! You would have had to look down on his balding head for the rest of your days."

She smiled. "I know not if I would have been able to resist rapping it on the odd occasion too. I'm sure it would have sounded quite hollow!"

Young Benedict caught Jack's attention from across the table and whispered far too loudly, "Father says if Clara cannot find a husband soon, she is to become a nun!" The boys giggled and squirmed delightedly, and Cedron merely frowned at their impertinence.

Juliet poured him more wine. "She's far too beautiful to be shut up in a convent."

"She's far too talkative!"

"Not all orders are silent. Make absolutely sure you have the right one, Father—take a *long* time searching."

"The one near Bury, where I'm bound for, is," Jack said, catching the boy's eye. "It's called the Convent of Saint Alba's Jawbone.

And the nuns there are very silent and very grave."

"Ha! Saint Alba's Jawbone. That sound's ominous—for Clara!"

"Yes, thank you for introducing that convent to my father, Jack!"

"Saint Elbow's Jawbone?" Benedict asked. And the boys began kicking each other and giggling.

"She'll be whipped daily for offences," Cedron laughed, "at least three times!"

"I will not! I believe I shall...I'll be a good daughter—as always—and go wherever you see fit, Father. However, I am not *begging* to go. Pray tell, why are they silent, Jack—any particular reason? And why her jawbone? What was remarkable about that?"

"She kept it shut, for a start!" Cedron said.

After the laughter died down, Clara said, "But do tell, Jack, what is the story behind it all?"

"I know only this much: she was a nun in a silent order, so it followed that she vowed never to speak, except in praising God. Then it happened that some marauding Vikings—or was it invading Normans?—nevertheless, this hoard of armed men ransacked the convent..."

"Well, they could hardly enter it in the proper sense," Clara said.

"Quit jesting, here comes the serious bit; they tortured Saint Alba to death, as they did with her entire convent. They played a game, to get the nuns to blaspheme, swear, or say anything other than their vows dictated. All the nun's folded speedily..."

"Who can blame them?" Clara said.

"...except." Jack held up his hand. "Except for Saint Alba—that's *Alba*, boys, not *elbow*!" The boys broke out in fresh giggling, and Jack finished his story. "They say she took days to die and never once uttered a sound. Her death was quite grizzly, I believe. I'll spare you the details of her agonizing last hours. But, in the years that followed this grizzly episode, the usual miracles began to occur, and she was duly canonized. When the bishop had her bones dug up for relics, they found that her jawbone had fused together."

"With a rose clenched in her teeth?"

"No, Clara," Jack laughed, "merely fused together."

Cedron raised his cup, "Well, the idea of having Clara's jaw fused shut is the most appealing thought spoken tonight."

Amid the hilarity, all three women present cried out their protests in unison: "Father!"

"Surely not, master!"

"My love! Don't!"

When the laughter subsided, Clara said, "Well, I have considered it—taking holy orders. But I'm not quiet enough, I suppose. I believe I'd be in trouble constantly, just as Father predicts. My existence would be miserable. I know it's not meant to be a merry old time, but ...well, I like the thought that someday I shall be a wife and a mother."

Jack moved back slightly, his eyes wide in mock alarm.

"No! Fear not, Jack! I could never marry a man I had no fondness for. Otherwise, my 'sharp tongue' would razor the poor fellow to death. For me it would have to be a love match, rather than for position or wealth." Then she muttered a little too harshly, "And you, poor fellow, have neither."

"Clara!"

Juliet smiled fondly at Cedron, placed her hand over his fist. "I know my husband loves me."

Clara clapped her hand to her brow. "Juliet dearest! I did not mean to imply that...and I don't think for one moment... Of course yours is the happiest of...anyone can see 'tis you my father loves, not Margaret."

The blood drained from Cedron's face. And Jack watched aghast as Clara desperately tried to talk her way to dry shores.

"It was a pageant. He merely played the part of husband to Margaret...that was a hilarious pageant! You should have been here to witness it, Jack! Brother Brendin nearly hanged himself properly, he played Judus so enthusiastically. Nay, it may have looked real, but 'tis merely friendship. It is merely that Margaret and Father lost their spouses in the same year, the same week, even. They've been close friends since; otherwise he would never have given her the earrings."

"What earrings?" Juliet asked.

"The ones that match your..." Clara touched her dress's neckline, then pulled her hand away as if burnt. "Only the goldsmith wouldn't sell them separately. Truly! I was there when he brought the set. I should have kept my eyes on the counter, but I happened to see...And perhaps it was too extravagant to give in one gift. I thought the earrings could have gone to Gwendolyn for her wedding—although she was married already—or..."

Juliet's knife clattered to the floor as she stood up and Clara's words petered out. All eyes fell upon the lady of the house. All but Cedron's. His left hand covered his eyes, his head down. Jack gazed at the signet ring on Cedron's little finger. Juliet's shaking hand reached for the pendant around her neck, and she tore it off with a vicious rip. She tossed it on the table, and it skidded and bounced across the thick wood, disappearing from sight as it fell to the floor.

"You cheating, lying, money-grabbing beast!"

"No, Juliet, it's not like...he's not...I tell you, they're only..."

Juliet turned on Clara and hit her hard across the cheek. The slap resounded through the stilted room.

"Tell me naught!" Then, with no sound other than the rustle of her skirts, Juliet left the room. The maid hurried after her in ghostly silence.

Clara held on to her smarting cheek.

Cedron rose up, and with two strides he'd crossed to her. Towering above her, he yanked her up out of her seat.

"You stupid, stupid wench!" he roared, landing back hand followed by flat hand, followed by back hand across her face.

She tried to scramble away but fell forward, knocking her chin on the table, and Cedron hauled her up again. She put her hand to her mouth; a bright flow of blood trickled down between her fingers like festive ribbons. Cedron ripped the pearl-encrusted comb from her head. Her hair, dark and tumbling, fell against her pale face, and he pulled and grabbled at her gown, ripping the neckline. Then he shoved her tripping and skidding to the door.

"You are no longer a child of mine! Get out of these fine things that my alliance with your stepmother has brought you, and put on your traveling clothes. Get out! Be gone from this house! You leave with nothing!"

Jack stared at his hands and stared at his hands—his closed, white-knuckled hands—while Cedron paced the floor, breathing heavily. He kicked over his chair and crashed his fist onto the table. Young Benedict slid down in his seat so low that only the top of his head showed, and his workmate cowered too.

At last Jack cleared his throat. "Well, I must be leaving for my sister's house before the night bell tolls." His voice was tight and quiet.

"She's no fit daughter of mine! No fit daughter! I want her dead! I want her worse than dead. Thrown out in the streets! Bridled! Aye! I'll have her bridled and thrown out! If I could rip her tongue from her mouth and tear it to pieces and leave her speechless for all eternity, so I would. I'll... Yes!" Cedron cried, "That's it! Worse than death, worse than a life in the gutter—a punishment for her nothing short of a living hell! Jack, what was that convent you spoke of?"

He waited for Jack's answer.

"*What was it?!*"

"The Convent of Saint Alba's Jawbone, Master Cedron."

"That's it—she's to go there! You take her for me, lad, as one last duty to your good master! I'll write out an application, entrust you with a dowry and all else, whatever is needed for you to deliver the girl to her well-deserved fate."

Chapter Three

She's pretty, but...

Clara couldn't understand why Jack was being so kind. He agreed with her father—she'd heard him. The way he grabbed her arm as he took her from her home showed how he loathed her. He snatched the bundle of clothes from the maid without allowing time for them to say their good-byes—and she would miss her. Oh, he was so rough and in such haste that night! And he wouldn't look her in the eye. And his hands were cold.

Each night she hugged her other, secret bundle. Their maid had scooped up her precious belt and wrapped it in a chemise. See—what a thoughtful, girl she was—and she had not had a moment to thank her. Clara did not take her purchase out. She closed her eyes and remembered, pictured it in her mind until she fell asleep.

Sometimes, during the day, she would hear Jack and his sister whispering in hisses about her. Oh, aye, he surely abhorred her. Yet he wouldn't leave her be. He came over to her side and made a show of being tender and thoughtful. Worrying about her eating, bringing her an egg. How did he expect her to eat with her mouth like that? Yet he insisted that she have something. He fed drops of beaten egg onto her swollen lips; did he not see how licking them up made her tongue bleed? And his sister peeping at them all the while. Clara was fierce glad to leave that little house; it made leaving Winchester easier.

* * * *

Jack delayed their departure as long as possible. He took Clara to his sister's house, where he was staying. They allowed her in, but did not look directly at her. They stole glances her way from across the room but avoided meeting her eyes. And apart from the most basic communications of politeness and hospitality, they had little to say to her. They pretended not to notice that her face was swollen and bloody, her manner full of shock and shame.

But at the earliest opportunity, Jack's sister cornered him.

"Who is she, Jack? Was this your doing?"

"Sooth, woman, certainly not!"

He assured her that Clara was not a kept woman, and explained that he had agreed to escort her to a convent near Bury. But he would say no more. He made up some straw bedding for her alongside his, and put up with his brother-in-law's glowering and his sister's hushed complaints: "Jack, it is good to have you visit here, but this is extreme, don't you think, bringing in a wench?" and, "You were supposed to leave yesterday!" and, "She'd better not be wanted. If I have the law knocking on the door, I'll never forgive you, Jack." And, "My husband will complain if she stays here another day. Jack, how long are you staying on?"

"Just until she's strong enough to travel. We'll leave in a day or so, I give you my word!"

He went to market and bought an egg and beat it up with milk, and fed it to Clara, drop by painful drop. She could barely open her mouth. He gave her a piece of cloth, dipped in lavender water, and helped her to wipe away the dried blood. Below her lower lip, her teeth had cut right through. Her tongue was savagely bitten—almost sliced in half. And she had a chipped tooth. Her nose had bled badly and was swollen too. Only Jack tended to her. His family left her alone, as though she were part of his baggage. Or a bad omen.

Clara didn't help any. She ducked her head, refused to look at anyone. For three days she huddled on her bedding, weeping quietly from time to time. Quietly. Jack didn't once hear her utter a word.

On the third morning, he woke before light. The straw bedding made him itch, even through his linen sheets. It was dark and stuffy. Four adults and a couple of kids were crowding the little room out. He heard Clara shift and scratch through her clothes. She had her back to him, and he leaned up on one elbow and whispered, "Clara, we'll go today, as soon as the gates open."

She said nothing. Slowly, she sat up and gave a faint nod.

Jack waited a moment.

"I don't think your father will...is going to..."

Clara swept her hands slowly across her eyes, as though rubbing the sleep away, and nodded again.

"Are you well?"

Nod.

"Does it ache?"

Another faint nod.

"You'll feel better once you're outside...out and about."

She turned to face him and looked as though she would smile, but of course she couldn't. Jack got up to get the fire going.

* * * *

The city walls glistened in the gray, drizzly morning. Lichen patches mottled the dark stonework. Ferns sprouted and slugs slithered out of the crevices. Despite it being summer, Clara shivered a little in the damp morning. She hoped that her soft boots would not let the rain seep in. When they passed through the gates, she pulled the hood of her traveling cape as far forward as it would go, so that her face was overshadowed. And she kept her head bent, hugging close to Jack. Other footsteps tromped about them, and cart wheels clattered nearby and a horse whinnied. Someone shouted, and Clara whipped round, as did Jack. But it was no one they knew. Naught to do with them. They continued through the shadow of the gate house. Its walls seemed to tower up endlessly, and the iron gate, fully drawn, hung above them in a menacing row of spikes. Savage, stark and black.

A few more times, as the city receded into the distance, Clara turned back to take another "last look" at her hometown. Walls, turrets, towers and rooftops blended into an unidentifiable muddle of grays and browns.

"Well, that's that then," Jack said. "Ever been this far out of the city?"

Clara shook her head.

"The air is pleasant, don't you think?"

She nodded.

"You're not hungry yet, are you? No? Good! We'll go as far as Leatherhead, if we can keep to this pace. There's a tavern there that serves a good soup; would you like that? I imagine you would." After a while, Jack added, "Tell me if I'm walking too fast for you."

But of course, she didn't.

They traveled most of the waking hours on their journey to Bury. Taverns were expensive, hostelries were uncomfortable, and a pessimistic reminder of Clara's destiny, and the alehouses tended to be boisterous. Besides, although it healed quickly and well, Clara didn't wish to show off her face. Her tongue had the worst scar. It now sported a bump, and she got into the habit of running it across the roof of her mouth. The bump felt enormous, and she kept her mouth shut as much as possible to hide it. The thin, red welt below her bottom lip made it look as though she were pouting.

And she was pouting, most of the time. This is what they all wanted from her, this silence. So silent she would be. She managed to keep up her wordless protest for a few days, trampling purposefully beside Jack with no thought for the comforts she was accustomed to. She deliberately sought out the crudest accommodation. It was all part of her great penance. It proved difficult to say, *Forget the barn; let us bed down in a haystack in that field!* without words, especially in the twilight, when expressions are hard to see. So, Clara began to talk. Grumpily at first, and only saying what was absolutely necessary.

Jack continued to be graciously kind towards her. "Are you sure you wish to sleep out? The barn is quite deserted."

"It's trespassing. The field is fine."

"It looks like rain."

"It always looks like rain."

"Clara, there is no need for you to punish yourself...nor me. *Clara!*" Jack strode after her as she stormed ahead into the dusk. "Could you not speak kindly to me, woman? I've done you no harm!" He hadn't, had he? He was merely the messenger—a servant. "I'm not *your* servant, Clara Baxter," he added quietly. "Do you consider yourself stations above me?" Were they not both children of craftsmen? He took her silence as the answer he feared, and felt less inclined to appease her.

But his words seeped in and softened her resolve. On the fourth day of their journey Clara gave up her silence altogether. It was an unusually sunny day. As they crossed over a bridge, the brook underneath gurgled temptingly to her, and she remembered her weekly visit to the stews. It felt like months since they'd started out, and her aching, sticky body cried out for the luxury of cleansing water—hot or cold. Her steps faltered. Jack was leaving her behind, striding on over the hump of the bridge.

"I'd love to wet my face," she said, "to bathe." She'd spoken to herself, so quietly that the sound of their footsteps should have drowned her words. But Jack stopped. He turned round, shrugged and opened his arms wide. "Then let's stop a while!"

He grabbed her hand and led her, tripping up and giggling, off the road and onto the bank. They crashed through the undergrowth, following the brook round a bend, to a more remote spot. Looking around to make quite sure they were alone, Jack pointed Clara to a spot in the stream just after the sharp bend, where some boulders and bushes would hide her nicely.

"I shall be just around the bend. Yell if anyone–anything–frightens you."

Clara nodded and shooed him away. Hurriedly, almost guiltily, she splashed about. She called out a few times, to check that he was still there, and he answered that all was clear.

The brook was icy cold, and she soon began to shiver. She rushed her bathing, rinsed her muddied clothes and scrambled out onto the bank. Birds chirped and fluttered in the leaves about her, and the long grass rustled in the tender breeze. Clumsy and awkward with shaking, Clara dressed in her change of clothes. They clung to her wet body, fighting every inch of the way, as she pulled and plumped, twisted and laced, until she was quite decent.

The air seemed like an oven blast after the freezing water, and the sunshine was so brilliantly hot that it felt like a solid weight on her back. She called to Jack, and after a moment he crashed through the brambles.

"That was heavenly!" she announced, although her teeth still chattered. "You take a turn–I'll wait where you were."

He stared after her as she spread out her wet clothes on a gorse bush before he turned to the brook.

Clara let her wet hair hang loose as she unfolded the chemise that hid her belt and gazed at the new purchase for a while. Then she packed it away again, and began to plait her damp hair. She heard Jack call out to make sure all was well, and she answered to reassure him.

Later, with the sun still burning down on their heads, they picked blackberries as they waited for their clothes to finish drying.

"Oh, what a glorious day!" Clara said. "I cannot remember when I last had such a wonderful time!"

Jack looked at her in surprise. "Aye. Perfect weather, good food, good company–what more could we ask for?"

Clara slid the bump of her tongue across the roof of her mouth and remembered why they were out in the middle of nowhere, enjoying nature's bounty.

"It's especially good to see you looking happy," Jack said.

"Oh, Jack! Bless you!" She said no more for some time.

* * * *

Jack thought it made her more elegant, this quietness. But the sting was that she seemed out of his reach now. More desirable, yet less obtainable. She did speak more than the first days, since the...injury. But although she spoke again—conversed—he could see her catch herself, stop mid-sentence, and become not only quiet, but still. He felt regretful, guilty even, that she had made this change for the better. This improvement in her character was like a scab, and toward the end of their journey, he couldn't resist picking at it.

"You're quieter," he remarked.

"As everyone wished I would be."

"You're not bitter, are you?" He nudged her. She nudged him back. Hard. He staggered, and she laughed. It was late afternoon, and the day was muggy. The sun had even managed to show its face again for an hour or two. Clara's hair glinted in the light. Wisps escaped from her plaits and framed her face in a soft haze.

Jack opened his mouth as though to say something, changed his mind and brushed a strand of hair from her cheek instead.

"Your hair has red in it."

"Never! 'Tis dark brown, like my mother's."

"But in the light some red shows."

They stopped as Clara folded her arms. "If anyone has red hair, it's you, Ginger!"

"Nay, not ginger. 'Tis the color of a good ale."

"You're either a bad poet or extremely thirsty!"

"That I am! Shall we make a detour? If we go left at yonder fork, in the distance, we can stop a while in Godwick; I worked there for a year or more. I know a house that sells an excellent brew."

Clara agreed readily, and they set off again. Although they made it to the fork in the road, they didn't get much farther before they came across an alehouse. The sun was now very low—and had crept behind an ominous bank of clouds—and it was getting damp and chilly.

"What say you we stop here for the night?" Jack asked.

Clara nodded and fastened her gimp around her face—even though she was an unmarried maiden, she wore it for traveling—it was safer that way.

"I fear my need for good ale has slowed us down."

"Jack, I can assure you, I have no qualms about delaying my arrival at the Convent of Saint Alba's Jawbone!"

Chapter Four

The alehouse was a crooked building, made of mud and daub with a thatched roof. It seemed large as they approached it from the outside, tramping along the spongy, muddy path. But at least a third of its size was the stables, and within the gray walls, it was narrow and dingy. It was a long, basic hall, with a loft space above for the landlord and his family. A large fireplace occupied the end farthest from the livestock.

Jack paused in the open doorway, hoping the landlord would turn him away on account of there being no room. For the house was heaving with rowdy soldiers. But the owner rubbed his sweaty hands together.

"You've arrived just in time for dinner, my good sir!"

As though he were afraid they might bolt, he speedily ushered Jack and Clara across the straw-strewn, earthen floor, to a space big enough for two to squeeze onto at the long trestle table. And a red-faced woman made sure they had a board and tankard each. The landlord filled them with ale, and with a curt nod and a wink, he set the jug down with a deliberate thud near Jack.

If the light was dull outside, it was worse indoors. The fireplace sported a large cauldron hanging on a chain above a good log fire, but it smoked badly and the room was not only dim, but hazy. The corky smell of spilt ale on wood, and the sulfurous hint of beans slowly cooking, rivaled with the scent of wood fire, sweat and a faint whiff of sweet dung.

Clara and Jack smiled apologetically as they wedged themselves between two battle-scarred men. The crowd was very noisy, shouting in a variety of male pitches across the table to each other, and swearing profusely as well. They were a jovial bunch, rather than brooding. The landlord plied them with ale, obviously intent on keeping it that way. There was also a group of minstrels, and the soldiers repeatedly called upon them to "make merry music!" Encouraged by the landlord with the promise of free board and a bottomless tankard if they complied with the troops' demands, the musicians happily obliged. And then, of course, there was the inevitable scattering of raucous wenches. It was hard to tell if they had arrived with the soldiers, or because of them. But they were there in full, with hair unfurling from wooden combs and bosoms popping out of their low necklines. Their cackling laughter was like intermittent cock crowing in a noisy farmyard.

Clara kept her gimp tucked tightly into place and sat, still and rigid, wedged between Jack and a soldier with crumpled ears. The soldier also had a scar running down the side of his face and across his chin, and, Clara noticed after a few minutes, one of his fingers was missing.

"But not one of the pair that counts!" He held up his two bow fingers in what, under different circumstances, would have been a rude gesture.

Clara made no reply. The soldier's eyes glinted as he stared at her for a while, before commenting, "Of course, I'm not as handsome as I once was..." He traced a finger down his scar. A pink earthworm, winding its way down his prickly cheek.

"Nay, nay! There's something appealing in a battle-weary face. Women respond to it. It has the same effect on them as that of a newborn baby."

Jack's knee nudged Clara's, and she might have taken the cue and held her tongue, but the soldier grunted and shifted himself to face her full-on.

"Ah, my good wench! So, you are not repulsed by this ugly old face?" His breath wafted in Clara's face, smelling of beer and rot.

"Nay!" she spluttered.

"Ugly!? Why, the man is hideous!" a mate called from the other side of the table and a deafening roar of laughter burst through the hall. And Clara caught the rueful look in her neighbor's eye, despite his lopsided grin.

"There be no such thing as an ugly face," she said, "'tis merely that some faces take a bit of getting used to. Your friend can find comfort in the fact that his rugged face is nevertheless interesting."

Luckily she wasn't the only tender-hearted woman present, and the eldest, least attractive of the wenches clamored out from her place on the bench, sauntered over to the scarred soldier, and laughingly suggested that he press his "interesting" face into her ample bosom to see if that would cure his ugliness. It didn't, of course, but as he hastened to point out, after some minutes of hooting and groping, it was a sure cure for poor spirits!

Dinner was served. It was the simple sort of food that Clara remembered from her childhood. A bean and vegetable stew served in pottage bowls and with the customary large slice of hard bread.

The stew had cooked slowly to a mouth-melting softness, with the ample garlic rendered sweet and inoffensive by gentle simmering. And the vegetables faded into dull, uninviting shades of browns, glassy creams and slate grays. In amongst these almost unidentifiable lumps, the dark little beans glistened, swollen fat and bursting out of their skins.

Although Clara sat next to Jack, the pottage bowls were arranged so that she was sharing with the scarred soldier. And he turned his attention to her once again. He topped up her tankard for her and gave her another lopsided grin. "A bit of meat would be welcome." His voice was gravelly, and the light of the table lamps twinkled in his eyes.

"Aye. A morsel of bacon is the perfect accompaniment to beans."

Jack nudged her again. She found it irritating that he listened in on every snippet of conversation. And then found what she was saying somehow offensive.

"I was thinking more of a handful of nice, firm breast," the soldier said.

"I thought men like the thigh..."

"Gwooohr! That we do, my young lass! That we do! Bit of nice, plump young breast in my face and juicy thighs round my waist."

Thoughtfully, Clara chewed and swallowed. Her eyes widened. "Oh. I understand you now."

"Bit of pudding round the back of the house, eh?"

"Ah, but you see, I'm not...I am a novice," she spluttered, her color deepening. "Indeed, I'm on my way to the Convent of Saint Alba's Jawbone. So I am off the menu, so to speak. Nay, you'll not like my breasts, they are not at all plump. They are better described as pert."

She received another, rather vicious, nudge from Jack.

"Gwoohr! Pert!" the soldier reeled.

"No, good sir! Indeed, I meant no such....besides, I've received a calling. The Lord has spoken to me, and I think we ought to obey His wishes! I must remain chaste. For my entire life. A condition, I imagine, which will prove easy, as I'll be cloistered away from handsome young devils like you." She paused to rub her smarting shoulder. "Yes, thank you, Jack! I shall indeed cease my prattling."

"What say you?!" The soldier nudged her from the other side. "I concluded that you were with the tailor. Trusted you were hankering after a bit of muscle...a good broad sword to replace his little needle?!"

Clara gasped and covered her mouth. Jack was listening, she could tell, even though he was staring at one of those fat little beans, stabbing at it with his knife.

The noise had dipped, and her words were heard across the length of the room as she hastened to correct the soldier, "No! No, you misunderstand me. This good man is merely escorting me. My father asked him to..."

A roar of laughter crashed over the table.

"A *tailor*; as an escort!" one soldier howled.

"Is this so?" another bellowed.

"How do you plan to defend her from cutthroat robbers and bandits? Wave your needle at them, eh? Darn them to death?"

Another wave of laughter cascaded over the table. Jack shrugged and smiled. Stabbed his vegetables and smiled.

"Now hear ye all, a scissors can be a formidable..." Clara began.

But the minstrel talked over her, "There's a song to be had out of that, for sure!"

"Pray listen, a scissors..." But another roar of laughter drowned her voice.

As the noise died down, Jack spoke, "With your presence along the roads, good gentlemen, there are no outlaws to speak of. 'My Lady' needed an escort only for decency's sake."

"And Jack is indeed very decent, are you not?" Clara put in. "Truly decent."

"Ah, but how do her parents trust you? You are, after all, a man, albeit a puny sort," a soldier pointed out.

"We do not have such an...attraction," Clara said. "We are as siblings to each other. Besides, I wish...ahem! I wish to become a bride of Christ. It's what my father demands, and I would never offend him again."

By now, the company had lost interest and gone back to their food, drink and previous conversations. All but Jack. He twisted the point of his knife into the table, watching the raw, pink wood showing up new and pale against the dark, dirt-ingrained surface. Without looking up, he nudged her again.

"I am wittering again, am I not?"

He nodded.

Clara ran her tongue along the roof of her mouth and felt the bump. She and Jack took a long swig from their tankards simultaneously. But neither noticed their mirrored movements. Neither spoke again, nor smiled, nor looked properly at another person for the rest of the evening.

Chapter Five

The following day was muggy and overcast, yet Clara squinted from the glare of the clouds as she tramped beside Jack towards Godwick. Her eyes ached, and her head throbbed, and by the grim look on his face, so did Jack's. The muzzy smell of damp earth and grass annoyed her. The country folk and their grimy brats staring up at them from their toil annoyed her. Their mangy dogs barked and their sheep stank. And there was hardly any bird song that she noticed. And the parting gift of fleas and lice from the alehouse riled her. And, as they'd been pushed onto the grassy verge on more than one occasion by pesky lords and knights on horseback, her skirt was dotted with ticks. She itched all over and gave up trying to be discreet about scratching. Thinking bitterly that Godwick town had better be worth the detour, she all but glared at Jack when she scratched. He hastily looked away.

"Godwick has serviceable public baths. I'll pay for you to go in, when we get there."

"Are you implying that I reek?" Clara snapped.

"Nay."

"Perhaps you are suggesting I look grubby?"

"I am not suggesting anything."

"Indeed? Because that's what it seems like. To me..."

"I merely noticed that you appear uncomfortable, Clara, merely that. But if you do not wish to..."

"Good. Thank you. I do not."

"Good."

"Good."

They walked on a little more in stony silence before Jack said, "Naturally *I* will. Indeed I am looking forward to a warm, cleansing soak."

Clara studied the horizon.

After a few paces Jack said, "The baths have been there since the Romans."

"Are they almost as good as Winchester's stews?"

"Better, by most accounts. Godwick has a small river running by it. And I know a market stall where they sell excellent infusions and soaps."

"The best ale, a perfect bathhouse, an excellent market...this Godwick sounds so wonderful, I cannot imagine why you ever strayed so far from this paradise."

Now it was Jack who seemed fascinated with the horizon.

"Well, why did you leave?" Clara asked.

"Ah! I...er...talk of the devil! Look ye yonder! There are the walls of Godwick!"

As they reached the brow of the hill, they could make out in the distance the familiar cluster of stone walls and turrets. It certainly was at least two sizes smaller than Clara's hometown, but it had a gate house and a strong wall around it, two roads meeting at its center, and a river for transport and water. Once they'd gotten to the point of having it in sight, they stepped up their pace, and their teasing ceased.

* * * *

Jack was beginning to regret passing through Godwick. As he got nearer he remembered all the bad things, all the irritations that had made his leaving easy. He noted, as he paid the guard at the toll gate, that the soldiers patrolling the walls and the gate wore the same emblem on their tunics and shields that they were sporting when he left. These were men loyal to Lord Arthur de Montfort.

If Clara did not have the energy to make derogatory comments about the streets being beaten earth as opposed to cobbled stone, he was glad of it. Both were worn out from the journey, especially from the last couple of miles. The market square was smaller than Winchester and the walk across town at least half the distance. But the river was not too dirty, and reeked only mildly of sewage and decay. Jack guided Clara on a winding path through its streets. Passing the castle, he brought her round to the common ground, which boasted a duck pond, pleasantly dotted with waterfowl, where children played around the edges. They left the green and passed the barracks and the newer, larger church. He pointed out the guild hall and the best houses before they rounded back toward the center of town, and the market square.

"We have three market days. On those days the common is crowded by livestock."

After leaving the market, they made an extravagant but worthwhile visit to the bathhouse. Next, Jack guided Clara through the built-up area of shops and houses, going down a narrow street towards his favorite tavern. The town was busy, but not heaving.

Jack took a deep breath, "I can pick out the baker's! Good old town smells, eh?"

"It's like being home, it smells so much alike. Smaller, perhaps, but not too small," Clara began; then she ran her tongue along the roof of her mouth and was quiet.

"They are all of one breed," Jack agreed, ducking slightly as he ushered her through the dark wooden frame of a tavern door. The long, dim room was beginning to fill up. Stools, benches and trestle tables, all of unfinished wood, smoothed down and darkened with use, gathered untidily in the dim room, with candlesticks, lanterns, and tankards at the ready. One or two regulars huddled motionless in corners by open shutters, clutching their mugs sleepily. The customary mixture of wood smoke and brew hung in the air.

From the depth of the gloom emerged a tall man. His teeth showed white in the shadows as he grinned, and his balding head gleamed. He wore a grimy apron over his tunic and another rag slumped over his shoulder. He spread his strong hands out and greeted them.

"Jack! Good Lord! After all this time!" He gripped Jack's shoulder with one hand as he shook hands with the other. "Where've you been, my man?"

Jack introduced him to Clara as Howard Claxton, and he sat down and drank with them, talking ceaselessly in a strong, resonating voice about all that had happened in Godwick since Jack left. Jack leaned forward to listen, making the odd enquiry about this person or that.

* * * *

Clara sat on the opposite side of the table. Content to rest, she leaned back and let the coppery ale dull her thoughts. Occasionally she was called upon to listen to some entertaining account, but she was glad to let the men become engrossed in catching up. Although their conversation was largely drowned out by the growing crowd of patrons, Clara caught a snippet of Howard's news that caused her to look up suddenly with a jolt.

"...indeed, he still hasn't married her. I believe she would be very glad to—"

"But I would not. I am only passing through. I am on my way

to Bury."

Howard glanced at Clara. She made a point of studying the remains of her ale, and he said, "Of course! But you'll be lucky to get away from Godwick just yet."

Jack and Clara looked at each other.

"How so?"

"Your coming here now is quite serendipitous—for the town," Howard said.

"Pray, do tell!"

"You will have noticed, I'm sure, that we are all a bit thin on the ground. We had a bad outbreak. Well, the thing is, Jack, that there's only one able tailor left in the whole town. Working his fingers to the bone, poor fellow."

"That is good for his business, is it not?"

"Not if he makes himself ill. Do you know what happened to your old master, Dermot?"

"Hmph! Him!" Jack scowled.

Howard leaned forward and licked his lips, "He has undergone a strange affliction. A very peculiar illness rendered him paralyzed on one side. Some say it is witchcraft; others say the wrath of God has come upon him. Regardless of its origin, the man is in a bad way now, unable to work. And his apprentice; my own son! The poor lad tried to finish Dermot's order for young Burke de Montfort, but of course it was no good. And de Montfort, being who he is, was not understanding. Ha! To say the least! Poor William was here, begging us to take him back home, and it looks as though we shall have to. My Matilda has sent them supper most nights of late."

Jack downed the last of his ale. "What a sad tale—you have my sympathy. But none of this is my problem. Not anymore." He stood up as if to go, and even as Howard opened his mouth to protest, a voice called from the doorway.

"They said you were here! Good man!"

Clara turned to see a high-ranking soldier—a comely man. Positively dashing, compared to the moth-eaten squadron in the alehouse! He had dark hair, brown eyes, a cleft chin and an air of confidence about him. Too much confidence. He had a bit of a swagger.

Jack's jaw tightened. "I'm just passing through, on my way to..."

"Not anymore. I'll get it in writing if I have to, but my uncle, Lord Arthur de Montfort, upon hearing of your timely arrival, has insisted that you remain in town. At any rate, until an adequate—and I emphasize *adequate*—tailor can be found. There is too much business for one tailor, especially if he be of Jewish origins. The other tailors could riot."

"But there is only *one* other tailor!" Jack cried.

"Aye, but his apprentice makes two. Admittedly, with his present affliction Dermot would simply walk in a tight circle, and William would undoubtedly sack the wrong shop. Pathetic as they are, other folk could rally together, and things may become riotous. Nevertheless, you are here. God sent, so to speak, and with my authority as town sheriff—"

"I'm already on a God-inspired quest. I have orders from this maiden's father to escort her to the Convent of Saint Alba's Jawbone."

Burke de Montfort turned and considered Clara. He looked her up and down.

"That is correct," Clara said. "It's a matter of urgency. Surrounded as I am by such charming men, I fear for my chastity."

Burke de Montfort winked. "I'm sure you do," he said, "but you can join the annual pilgrimage to Saint Alba's. It surprises me Jack never told you that. You have less than a fortnight to wait for it to march through the walls of this very town, and on right into the very heart of the convent. Until then, fair maiden, you shall have my protection."

He bowed and turned his attention to Jack. "I trust you have not been stringing the poor wench along, you dark horse!"

"Nay, never!"

The two men locked eyes for a moment; then, squaring his shoulders, Burke said, with a brisk tap on Jack's chest, "Very good! You are to take up lodgings and *journey* work at old Dermot's, and you, fair maiden"—he took Clara's hand in his, brushing his lips across it as he finished—"you wait here to join the Saint Alba's pilgrim."

He gave her another wink, with a click of his tongue, and strode out.

"But, where...but how long..." Clara turned to Jack and Howard. "Does he truly mean for me to stay here? In this tavern?"

Howard opened his mouth to speak, but Jack cut in abruptly.

"Nay. You shall accompany me!" He took her arm and led her out into the street.

Rather roughly, she felt.

"What is in this ale that makes the men of Godwick so brazen?"

she protested, vainly trying to wriggle free of his grasp.

"It pleased you, did that?" Jack growled in her ear as he steered her down the street.

"I beg your pardon? What, precisely, do you refer to?"

"All that winking and banter with Sheriff Burke de Montfort."

"No, indeed! 'Twas *he* who winked at *me*. That is all. I have a calling, remember, and shall remain chaste! I imagine he pursues all young women thus!"

Jack stopped and pointed a finger at her. "Never forget that, Clara! If I merely see one hint of such...bosom banter unfolding between you and that Burke, I'll...I'll..."

"Aye? You shall what, Jack?"

"I'll...I'll tell a nun."

"Oh. Aye, I see. You have me in a strong hold, there."

Jack bowed slightly, and they fell in step.

"'Bosom banter!' My, how quaint Godwick's English is!"

* * * *

Jack ignored her grandly and led the way until they reached the three-story, jettied house where he lived and worked for well nigh two years. It was narrow, squashed between two other buildings. All with blackened support beams, four pokey windows and tiled roof. But this house, he felt, was uglier. Perhaps it leaned a little too much to the one side, or the whitewash was grayer—he could detect a dog's pee stain on the wall near the doorway. Or was it just Dermot's energy emanating from within? He sighed and gave an elaborately grand bow. "I give you the humble abode of Dermot the tailor!"

It was lost on Clara, he perceived bitterly. She was too taken with greeting the occupants leaning out of the shop opposite. The tailor, Gimmer. The man, his wife and two young boys returned her wave amicably. Their shelves were down for business and their fabric on display. Unlike Dermot's house, which was shut.

"That is the competition you are greeting so courteously. Well, shall we step inside?"

The bell rang as he shoved the ill-fitting door open.

"Who is it?" a frightened voice squeaked from the gloomy back of the shop. Jack threw open the wooden shutters, and streams of light poured in. There was the usual furniture to be found in a tailor's workshop. The deep workbench—over which Jack had to lean to open the shutters—ran across the width of the room. It was littered with off cuts, an unfinished tunic, a stale pie crust, a leather tankard, two pairs of scissors, and a scattering of needles. Two crudely made wooden chests cluttered up the far end of the room, where a narrow staircase led to the living quarters. A wooden rail hung with a fine linen smock stretched overhead. A long, narrow table with more litter, including four burnt-down candles and a lamp, stood off to one side. And a couple of low stools—one of them lying on its side—made up the rest of the furnishings.

"We are not open!" a thin little boy insisted, lingering at the foot of the staircase, one foot on the first stair and his hand on the rope railing. His eyes were round and wide, making his pointed little chin and button nose seem tiny. His narrow fingers fidgeted, and he looked as though he might take flight at the slightest provocation.

"We are not customers," Jack said.

The boy's eyes looked heavenward. "Thank the Lord!"

Clara rushed forward and reached out a comforting hand. "You poor dear child! We have come to help you. The sheriff, er... Burke de Montford sent us."

The boy's face had begun to relax at the first of her words, but the anxiety was quickly rekindled.

Jack put a gentle hand on the lad's shoulder. "Do not fear, lad—he shall no longer trouble you for his jerkin. I've come on his orders to be Dermot's journeyman. And this is Clara—she's going to stop here for a number of days. As...as a housekeeper."

"You must be William. I'm on my way to the convent of Saint Alba's Jawbone. I'm going to be a novice."

William blinked.

A thump and a knock resounded from upstairs, and an old man's voice cried down, "William! I told you not to take any more customers. Be gone! I am a sick man!" An exuberant coughing spasm followed.

Jack sighed and, pushing past William, took the steps two at a time. "Dermot! It is I. Jack Paisley."

* * * *

Clara and William followed. Upstairs was worse by far than downstairs. The rasping sent of stale urine hung thickly in the musty air. Here too, the shutters were closed, and Clara tripped over a pair of smelly shoes, stumbled into a chest, and kicked something that went "*thunk*" and sloshed suspiciously like a full chamber pot as it slid across the wooden floor. But at last she got to the shutters and flung them open. Leaning out into the thinner, fresher air outside, she breathed deeply before turning to take in the room.

Its fireplace was full of ashes that should have been put out ages ago, and the cooking utensils were scattered around it, rather than actually working in it; a cauldron and a pair of firedogs, a kettle and a saucepan. A couple of boards and tankards and a chandelier loitered on what should have been a fine chest of drawers. A trestle table, once again a mess with ring stains, another board and a dirty knife, and bowls. A stool with a candlestick and a jug on it stood beside what should have been an impressive four-poster bed. But its curtains were torn down, and the woolen blankets that lay crumpled over it were stained and smelly. And in that bed lay the tailor, Dermot. His gray hair was limp and stringy, and his brow shone with grease. His prickly chin was encrusted with old pottage, or scabs, or both. His pale lips were dry and his cheeks were hollow, but his blue eyes sparkled vividly beneath graying caterpillar eyebrows.

At first he howled when daylight streamed in, but when his eyes focused on Clara, his protests faded into sounds of delighted surprise.

"Ah! Have I died and gone to Heaven, or is that indeed an angel come to nurse me?" He spoke out of one side of his mouth, and his speech was slurred and unclear. William had obviously been trying to get the old man to eat some broth. He came now to his side, picked up the little wooden bowl, and held out a spoonful. Dermot did nothing to help. He tried to slurp off of the spoon whilst still lying on his back. The broth dribbled all over, and he choked. He slapped out at William. "Too much! Too hot!"

William sat back on his haunches and sighed pathetically.

"Make haste, feed me! Before it cools again!"

Clara moved forward. "Here, allow me. You are both tired, and this is a woman's work. Now, lift up your head," she said, putting an arm around Dermot's shoulders to try and lift him to a sitting position. His head lolled onto her breast, and he slid over until he was leaning heavily on her. Jack quickly fluffed up the straw in the mattress to make a pillow for Dermot's head and back. The straw was old and about as uncooperative as Dermot. Jack kept his arms behind the mattress, holding it upright. Clara, meanwhile, took a spoonful of broth while William held the bowl, and Dermot took it down beautifully.

"There, now!"

William smiled.

Jack shook his head. "I am dumbstruck! Three people to feed you, Dermot. You must feel like a king!"

"Ah, it would be so, if you were all women!" Dermot's good hand flopped onto Clara's lap. Jack gave the mattress a rough shake. He told William to fetch a low stool and used that to prop up the mattress. Dermot complained that it was too upright, but swallowed down the rest of the broth.

"Well, Jack, why have you returned to your old master? And why do you present me with this scrumptious gift, eh?" He tried to take Clara's hand, but she moved swiftly out of the way, taking the bowl to a bucket on the table.

"I was ordered to. And Clara is not here for your benefit."

"Oh, I am keen to assist these good people. However, I am only here for a short time. I am on my way to the Convent of Saint Alba's Jawbone, to take up the position as a novice."

"Oh aye, I fancy a bit of a nun! You can practice your healing skills on me!" Dermot's voice lowered, and he held out his hand imploringly. "I suffer terribly from a mysterious affliction. None other than a woman of God can cure me, now."

Jack groaned and put his head in his hands, "Nay, but this will never work! I cannot keep you here, Clara. This is not a patch on what you are accustomed to. And with Dermot performing..."

"Nonsense! It can't be worse than any of the barns and alehouses we've stopped at so far. Besides, this place needs a woman's touch..."

"Aye, I need the touch of a woman!" The old man cackled and eyed her from his bed.

Clara stepped closer to Jack.

"This may be a good opportunity to get an understanding of the nursing work I shall be expected to manage..."

"Saint Alba's is a closed order—I hardly think you'll be doing much nursing."

"And I recall when our house was small and simple too," she said, ignoring his interruption.

"For pity's sake, Clara! It will take a year's work and a year's worth of salary to improve this hellhole!"

"But nay! One day's labor will be time enough. And as a show of confidence in your work, I shall lend you what you need to set up home here from the dowry my good father provided to enter the convent."

"It is not yours to give."

"*Lend,* Jack, lend. And pray tell, who's to know?"

"I shall know. Besides, I have no need to borrow money from you." Jack glared at her and pulled his pouch from inside his gypon and threw it on the table. "There are my savings, to buy materials for my masterpiece. Take that and use it; my guild money!"

"It shall soon be replenished," Clara insisted. "If you cannot trust in God, then at least remember that the town needs you. Its people love you and want you here. Surely they will support you? And how can we ignore the plight of this little house." She took his hands in hers. "Poor little William needs a mother's presence. I'll turn this into a pleasant home and keep house while I remain. As I care for Dermot, you will be free to peruse the business of tailoring with vigor. I believe—and pray with all my heart—when the time comes for me to leave, you'll have earned back your money and made more. You can; you know you can!" She stepped away from him, letting his hand linger for just a moment longer in hers.

"Aye. Your word is true. We have no choice, as it is." He rubbed his forehead. "Right! William, you are to help Clara with cleaning upstairs, and I shall get the shop in order. Do not—upon my word—do not, either of you, attempt to sort Dermot and his rancid bed out until I'm here to help!" He gave the old man a warning look before bounding down the narrow stairs.

Clara and William stared grimly at each other for a moment.

"Well," she said, rolling up her sleeves, "take the bucket, William, and fetch us some water!"

It took several buckets of water—each one emptied out almost black—and the whole day of shifting, scrubbing, sweeping and wiping to get the room in order. But Clara and William worked with might and main, and by the end of the first day the second floor was clean, bright and neat. The trestle table was scrubbed and the crockery packed away between meals. The fireplace was clean and in good working order.

Chapter Six

While cleaning the house, Clara made two discoveries. The first one was that Dermot was not entirely bedridden. Jack had gotten him out of bed so that they could give him a fresh straw mattress. He was supposed to be leaning upright on William, when he took two steps to reach Clara and tried to get his arm around her as she shifted the mattress into place. Without thinking, she stepped away to avoid him, and he took a further two steps before Jack sprang to her rescue.

"No, you don't!" He grabbed Dermot under the arms, heaving him onto the bench.

"He meant no harm," Clara said.

Ignoring her, Jack turned on Dermot. "Why did you keep from us this secret that you can walk?"

Dermot slid down in his seat slightly, adopting a crooked stance, and gazed from one to the other like a forlorn mutt. "I can hobble but a few steps. Besides, you never inquired if I could walk!"

"Jack, I believe you misread the poor man's intentions."

"I most certainly did not!"

They let the argument lie at that. There was a fireplace to clean and floors to sweep. Clutter to be cleared, drawers and chests to tidy. Jack was called up three times to demolish mice nests and evict the respective lodgers as they were found.

"We need a good mouser," Clara muttered more than once. She scrubbed all the surfaces and scrubbed them again, despite the cost of water and soap. A rag and bone man took what needed to be thrown out, including a pile of desiccated meal remains that Clara dug out from behind the drawers.

On the third floor, the smallest room was used only as an attic. Jack helped Clara set up two straw mattresses in it, and William gave over his little truckle bed to Clara. Jack helped them haul it up to the third floor, and they set up a curtain from a rat-nibbled linen sheet that Clara pulled from a chest in the room. Other things that came out of it—candlesticks, some forgotten candles, and a pair of sheets—were all put to good use.

Clara's second discovery was a cradle, complete with its linen and some baby clothes, all packed away, hidden behind the chest in the darkest corner of the room. She stared at it for a while, and then quietly tucked it back into its hidey hole.

She and William went out and purchased fresh bedding, more firewood, more candles and a barrel of cider, a barrel of flour and one of beans. She purchased some honey, herbs, and seasonal vegetables, bacon and an egg for Dermot.

At last, with the sun low and the streets below emptying, Clara looked around the solar and sighed.

"It's as though we are in a different house," William remarked.

"Aye, 'tis true! If I didn't have such aching limbs and rough hands, I would be convinced that we were!"

When the table—still damp from cleaning—was properly set for four, and Jack stood in the doorway with a pie he'd bought with his last grout, Clara insisted that Dermot sit at the table and join them for dinner.

"Naw! Let me be; I can eat in bed!"

Clara put her hands on her hips. "Nonsense! I will not have you messing food on that nice new straw!"

The old man glared back at her. "If you want me out, then you get me out!"

Jack hurriedly plonked the pie on the table, but before he could reach Dermot, Clara stormed across to the invalid and led him speedily to the table, dumping him on the stool while pushing his hand away from her breasts.

"See?" Jack said grimly, arms folded, "I'll wager you would walk unaided through the entire town if Clara danced naked in front of you!"

Dermot's eyes lit up.

"Hush, Jack!" Clara poured ale out for them all in turn, from a newly cleaned and sparkling pipkin.

"Would you like a sip now, Dermot?" she asked kindly and lifted the mug to his mouth. He sucked eagerly at the amber liquid, its creamy head settling on his upper lip, as his good hand crept towards Clara's breast in an attempt to cup it.

"Take heed!" William warned, pointing as she, sensing something amiss, jumped back. Dermot lunged with his free hand, the other still clasped around his tankard. Ale sloshed out, spilling on Clara's top—on her left breast—and settled there as they all stared at Dermot.

"He meant no harm! You were surely trying to hold your own

drink, is that not so, Dermot?" Clara said at last.

William and Jack exchanged looks.

"Aye, I was," he slurred in a frail voice. And he took a clumsy sip from the tankard, a dribble of ale trickling down his chin.

"Hark!" Clara cried, all but clapping with enthusiasm, "Dermot can hold a tankard in his right hand, and put it to his lips. Dermot, it appears you are improving! Let us see if you can pick up your spoon and put it to your mouth."

"*I* shall assist," Jack said sharply, and leaned over. A little gruffly, Dermot shooed his hands away after the first mouthful and began eating by himself.

"Bravo!" Clara cried. This time she did clap, and Dermot looked from one face to the other, beaming happily.

"I had a notion he could," William muttered darkly.

"It must be a sign from God!" Clara enthused.

"A miracle," Jack replied dryly, and drained his tankard.

"Truly!" Clara got up from her seat to come over and pour more ale out for him. "All will be well, Jack, you'll see!"

Their eyes met, and the pipkin faltered for an instant in her hand. She grasped at the belly of the jug, and her fingers brushed against his. His gaze intensified, searching.

"Clara..." But even as he opened his mouth, there was a rapping at the door.

"Customers!" William squeaked, cringing.

Clara dumped the pipkin down and reached up to tidy her hair.

Jack eyed the stain on her breast. "I shall answer it," he said, lifting his long legs over the bench and striding to the staircase. Clara and William hovered at the top of the landing, watching him open the door.

"We are closed...oh..."

He stepped back, opening the door wide. In its frame stood a young woman. Her hair was uncovered and set up in golden plaits. Her eyes were wide and blue, and her lips were full and red. Her skin was fair and her dress draped softly over her curves.

"I bid thee good day, Jack." She stepped lightly over the threshold. "No tailor ever sewed a seam quite as neat as you; so when I heard you were back, I hastened here to place an order. And I've brought you this." She held up the jug, and lamely Jack took it.

"Oh. Thank you...er...that is indeed kind."

"Oh, it is not from me. I'm merely the messenger. Howard has sent it to you. He and Miriam are very glad to have William under your instruction now." She tilted her head gently and gazed at him through thick lashes.

For a moment no one spoke.

At the top of the stairs, Clara mouthed to William, "Who *is* she?"

He looked helplessly from one woman to the other and back again, and clutched his hands together.

"Good," Jack said at last.

The woman looked past him now, through the back of the shop and up the stairs.

Clara swallowed hard, lifted her chin and started down. The rope swung precariously as she clutched at it, causing her to stumble forward. Her descent was rapid and clumsy. She smoothed her skirts even as she regained her balance at the foot of the steps, and then lifted her chin again.

The woman looked her quickly up and down before offering a brief smile. She arched her brows and turned to Jack. "You have a servant?"

"Er...housekeeper." He scratched his head. "Clara, this is—"

"Nun!" Clara blurted out. A short, starched silence followed. "That is, I will be a nun. Shortly. I shall become a novice aspiring to be a nun. I am waiting for the Saint Alba's pilgrimage. I will join that and...then join the Convent of Saint Alba's Jawbone."

"I see."

"But in the meantime I am keeping house for Jack."

"I see."

Jack cleared his throat. "I know Clara's father, Mr. Cedron Baxter. He is a tailor and a merchant in Winchester. I agreed upon his request to escort Clara to the convent."

"Ah! I see!" The other woman came forward. "Clara, is it? I am Ingrid, an...er...old friend of Jack's. And we will surely be great friends too. For your short stay here."

"Oh," Clara said in a small voice as she took the smooth, cool hand offered. Her own hand was coarse and red. "I've been cleaning," she mumbled apologetically.

"So I see," Ingrid said, looking around, "It is very much improved!"

"This is Jack's work," Clara said hastily, "I cleaned upstairs. Would you like to come and see? You'll find such a difference. Come up, if we are to be friends. What I mean to say is, I should like that—very much. Have you seen it before—upstairs?"

"Yes, verily so! Many times! When Jack resided here," she replied airily. She offered her hand to Jack.

"I see," Clara mumbled, hanging back as they swept upstairs.

Following behind Jack and Ingrid, Clara grasped William's arm. "How well did they know one another?"

William shrugged. "I know not, Miss Clara."

"Well, no one talks of it, do they?" she asked. He shrugged again but was prevented from replying properly, as they'd reached the solar.

"My! This is very homely." Ingrid's gaze swept the room. "I almost expected to see a cradle."

Clara looked dumbly upwards.

Ingrid laughed as her eyes rested on her. "And especially as your left breast appears to be leaking!"

"What?" Clara looked down and found the dark, wet stain. "Oh!" She wiped at it fruitlessly. In her panic she tried to lick it to taste it and see what it was, but her tongue couldn't reach. She licked her fingers instead. "Oh, but of course, fear not! It is merely ale," she sighed. Her relief slipped away as, looking up, she saw everyone staring at her. Their expressions ranged from blank to amused dismay.

"It is ale!" she snapped. She felt her face grow hot. "It must be from when Dermot spilt... Oh, Dermot can hold a tankard now. Ingrid, did you know?"

"Ooh, aye, but I'd much rather drink my ale from a woman's breast!" Dermot growled, his face pink and his eyes shining.

The women shrieked, drowning out Jack's barked objection, and it was a full minute before their hysterical laughter ceased.

"He's a harmless old dear! He is a little...that is...he truly does not know what he implies...he means no harm. "

"Surely not." Ingrid grinned, with a very familiar wink. "And yet, I would keep him at an arm's length if I were you! Well, I must away! Jack, would you take my measurements before I go? So nice meeting you, Clara! I can tell we're going to be tremendous friends!"

Clara watched them as they went down the stairs together. Her eyes narrowed, and she let out a smothered cry of frustration, and whipped round to face Dermot and William.

"Thank you very much, gentlemen! Why did you not inform me?"

"Eh?" Dermot, seeming suddenly very benign, pivoted himself round clumsily and peered anxiously at her.

"I beg your pardon, miss," William squeaked.

"This!" she snapped, indicating her left breast, which had

begun to itch uncomfortably from the damp. "Hark at this! Why did you men say naught of it earlier? Jack could have warned me."

"Eh?"

"We...we didn't notice, miss!"

"Typical!" Then, seeing the apprentice's bottom lip quiver, Clara closed her eyes and took a deep breath. "No, of course you did not. I apologize."

Dermot, losing his already fragile sense of balance, tumbled off his stool, onto the floor. He lay there as still and silent as a rag doll.

"What a poor nurse I am," Clara sighed. "I cannot see that I will be a good nun!"

Chapter Seven

The next morning, Clara woke to find that Jack was up before her and had already gone down to the shop. She took him some bread and ale. He'd thrown open the shutters, letting the blue dawn light wash the room. He was already cutting out Ingrid's sleeves. The scissors rasped, slicing through the stillness of the new day in a steady rhythm. It was a sound she knew from her earliest childhood, and she stopped dead to hear it again. She stood in the doorway, watching the movement of his hand as it commanded the tool of his trade. The strong knuckles of his thumb and fingers jutted out in white, angular mounds as his hands worked the scissors. The veins running down the back of his hand wound in contrast to the straight fan of tendons, visible in the pulsing motion of cutting. His face, as he worked, was serene despite the tension in his mouth. His eyes were intense with focus as he cut. Then the scissors met the beginning of its path, and the tone changed abruptly, becoming a sharper, thinner rasp, as the blade found no fabric to bite. Jack blew lightly at the severed fibers and stood up. He looked at Clara, acknowledging her presence for the first time since she'd entered.

"I brought you some breakfast...perhaps you'd like..." She found her words inexplicably catching in her throat, her heart beating and her cheeks burning as their eyes met.

Jack pointed with the scissors to the stool he'd placed by the tiny fireplace. "I'll have it over there. Thanks."

Feeling melancholy for some reason she couldn't quite catch, Clara placed the board on the stool and left the room. As she reached the stairs, Jack called her back.

"Clara! Er... Is Dermot well?"

She turned back, her face blank.

"After his fall last night—is he better?" He moved toward her.

"Oh. Yes. He is fine. He is still snoring. Methinks we gave him too much ale. Perhaps we should ensure he drinks no more than half a tankard. Or we could ask Howard for a lighter brew."

"Both!"

He invited her to share in his breakfast, and they chatted until

William, returning from an early errand, breezed in happily.

"I've told everyone I know you are here, Master Jack," he grinned, "and many remembered you. They said they shall be round to do business."

"How kind of them! We'll make our fortune!"

"Don't be so ungrateful!" Clara gasped.

Jack stroked his chin. "I smell a rat, though. Why would the community here be so supportive?"

"Because you inspire love wherever you go. Because they all liked you and missed you. Because the town's desperate for another tailor, and your work has a good reputation."

"Mr. Elwood the cloth merchant looked very pleased," William said. "He sends his regards and hopes to see you soon."

"Perhaps he'll allow me some credit," Jack said, but he shook his head. "I cannot help but feel there must be a better motive for them to kidnap me like this."

Clara and William made no reply to that.

"And I do believe," he finished after a moment, "that the truth shall be revealed before the day is out. Anyway, if we are to have a queue of customers beating a path to our door, we'd better put our nose to the grindstone! William, how good is your tacking?"

"I can help, if you need me," Clara offered, gathering up the board and empty tankard.

Both of Jack's assumptions were proven right; there was an ulterior motive to his being in such demand, and they discovered it before the day was out.

Business was good; old customers came in to ask for fittings, and a few old friends came in to chat. However, Jack was forced to keep it very short and arranged with each one to meet up in Howard's tavern after the day's work.

"I really should be working into the night, rather than socializing," he said to William. "Business is almost too good. I'll have to pay Mr. Elwood a visit first thing in the morning."

But when the evening drew near, he stretched until his hands touched the beams. His back cricked as he twisted left and then right.

"Howard's ale beckons me, William. Finish what you're busy with, then sweep up. I'll be back within the hour." He called up the stairs, "Clara! Come and drink some ale with me!"

And he explained, as she laced her pattens on, "Your company will ensure that I do not linger too long."

"How charming you are!" she grumbled.

He led her out into the street in the evening sun, disturbing an enormous tabby cat as he pulled the door shut. It spat viciously at them before slinking away. The crowds were thinning; most people were homeward bound. A baker's boy hurried past with the last of his delivery; lovers touched hands as they lingered in the doorway of a shop. Up on the walls, the armored soldiers on patrol looked down on the townsfolk with idle suspicion and prepared to change guard. And approaching the gates, the visitors and travelers quickened their pace as the keeper jingled his keys teasingly.

Clara dodged and ducked her way behind Jack's long stride. She arrived at the tavern panting and irritable, bumping into him as he stopped abruptly at the doors to let another customer pass out.

"I am wasting good daylight." He scowled at the darkening gray skies.

"Such as it is," Clara said. "And if you keep up this pace as you have your drink and repartee, we shall be out again in two shakes of a duck's tail."

He took in her red face and her angry eye. "You're right. I've come now, and I shouldn't grumble."

He escorted her through the crowded room, his eyes scanning the herd of hunched shoulders for the familiar shapes of his old pals.

"Ah! There they sit!"

Clara squeezed up between Jack and a blond fellow who was eating bread and cheese. She sipped her cloudy cider and listened in on their reminiscence. Howard Claxton came and stood by their table for a while, joining in the increasingly loud conversation. His wife appeared too, on and off, often carrying tankards of ale and making urgent eye contact with Howard. Her wimple was crooked, and ash-gray strands of hair escaped across her cheeks. And Jack's rival in business, the tailor Richard Gimmer, came along, looking expectantly through the growing crowds. Laughter crashed across the tables like waves over a rocky beach, and the occasional loud whoops and jeers rang sharp and clear through the jabbering of the customers. And Clara's head began to swim in the confusion of the noise and the cloudiness of her cider. She looked up to see Ingrid beaming at her from opposite the table, and blinked.

"Ingrid?"

"Methinks you may be glad of a woman's company!"

"Thank you. Did you seek me out especially?"

Ingrid indicated the crowded table. "No. We always meet up here." She leaned across and nudged Jack. She touched his hand. "Like old times, eh?" She laughed.

Clara smiled woodenly and leaned back, apart from the happy crowd. When Howard's Matilda said, "Ah, here he is at last!" the table hushed.

A short man carrying something under his cape picked his way through the room to their table.

"Good evening, Simon!"

"Jack!" He beamed. They all parted, making a space for him to sit next to Jack, "You are just the man we need."

Jack looked from one familiar face to the next. "Aye?" he asked slowly.

"I have spent many hours," Simon embellished, to the nodding appraisal of their well-rehearsed companions, "making this fine Toole hand"—here he playfully caught Clara's eye, and whipped the construction from under his cape—"crafted lovingly with these hands of a joiner. Carved out of the best wood....the sacred hand of Saint Toole! Well, a replica thereof." He chuckled quietly, the tips of his ears glowing. His companions eyed the hand expectantly. It was a very crude wooden frame of an outstretched hand and wrist. It bore no joints and therefore had no movement. It seemed to be supported by not only one rod to hold it up, but a few thinner, additional rods. It was a very peculiar hand.

"Of course, I know it's not as good as the old one," he said. "But it's different, you see."

"Exceedingly different!" Howard snorted.

Jack scratched his head. "But what became of our fine olive-wood hand?"

"Why, Jack, have you not heard?" Ingrid asked, her eyes glistening beautifully. "It was burnt in a fire three years ago. Burnt to cinders!"

"Treachery!" Howard muttered, and a man beside him spat onto the rushes.

"A fire?" Jack asked, "How so?"

"No one knows. We've had no justice, no justice at all," Catherine said, adding bitterly, "not with the coroner belonging to the Palmers' Guild."

"Such a shame!" sighed another.

Jack stared at the hand Simon the joiner offered, and his assembled friends followed his gaze.

"Well," Simon asked at length, "what say you?

Jack took a deep breath. "It needs a little filling out," he ventured. "But otherwise, it's very good."

"It needs a great deal of filling out!" one man said.

"It looks skeletal!" another declared.

But this remark, rather than offend, seemed to please Simon the joiner. "That's where I—*we*—thought you could help, Jack,"

"Ah, nay. Nay, never!" Jack shook his head. "If you could not make this look more hand-like, then I could fair no better."

"But you could!" more than one voice cried.

"Never! I cannot carve wood!"

Howard put an arm round his shoulders. "We have no intention to reproduce the old one at all. We have a desire to make something quite different, quite new. Would you not say that this makes a fine *frame* for a hand?"

Jack hesitated. "I expect so, aye."

Everyone looked at him expectantly.

"I...er...a covering would finish it off, mayhap? "

"Exactly!"

"But surely that's a job for the glove maker?" he asked.

"Alas, we have but one glove maker left in Godwick, and he's with the Palmers' Guild, you see."

"The tanners, then?" Jack tried again. "Leather is far better wearing than anything in linen or silk."

"Same with them," was the tight-lipped reply.

"And I cannot see how you even consider asking them; why, we believe they had a hand in the fire," Matilda pointed out.

"No, it has to be a tailor's work," Howard insisted, pouring Jack a fresh tankard.

"Exactly!" Jack said. "Why has Robert Gimmer not begun a cover for the hand yet?"

"The task has sat with him for two months now. He is too bound down with orders, overloaded with work, to even begin."

"Besides," Ingrid put in, eyeing Jack from under her thick lashes, "your sewing is speedier, and better, than his."

The joiner added, "He'll gladly provide the materials. Indeed he has some set aside."

Jack leaned back slightly. "I'm very flattered, but I—"

"Ah, Jack, me boy!" A voice rang out from the doorway of the room.

A priest, clad in a dark habit, came pushing through the crowds.

"Ingrid swore that you had returned, although I had mind to

doubt her. I had to come for myself and see."

Howard signaled to his barmaid, and she came over with a pipkin and a tankard.

"Nay, no, not for me," the priest said unconvincingly, "I'm on my way to visit a sick bed—I fear I cannot stop. I have been tending the parish all this long day! I have two mothers crying out for their babes to be baptized, and everyone wants to take confession in preparation for Saint Toole's day. I'm verily glad to have a reliable helper back, Jack. I have been attempting in vain for months to get the hand finished..." He inspected the joiner's work as he spoke. "Yes, indeed...we urgently need to get it finished. I do not wish to endure the scorn of the nuns of Saint Alba's Jawbone again." He leaned closer to Jack. "Last year they overran our parade. We were wholly overshadowed. Eclipsed, I tell you! Cursed palmers' monks!"

And thus the priest launched into a long-winded gripe. "I recommend a pilgrimage to purge the soul, but to arrange the Saint Alba's march to coincide with Saint Toole's day is ungodly competition. Their march cuts straight through my territory, like a knife. And on the exact same day! They could arrange it to be a week or so later, surely!"

All but Clara now avoided his eye. Seeing she was a willing audience, he fixed her with his attention.

"Greetings! I'm Father John; are you new to this town?"

"I am with Jack, but I am only passing through. That is, my father asked him to escort me. I'm going to enter the convent of Saint Alba's Jawbone... Oh, but I am thereby cast on to the other side, am I not? I know naught of it, nothing of it... I beg of you; do not consider me an enemy! Not that I am disloyal... I mean, I am here with Jack—as my escort—until I go. And until then can I side with you?"

"To be sure," Ingrid said, "any friend of Jack's is one of ours."

Clara frowned. "I didn't know you were all against Saint Alba. Was she not a good saint? Jack told me about her. She seems quite holy..."

"I've nothing against her as a saint," Father John said, "it is the nuns that vex me so!"

"Oh, dear!"

"Well, the nuns and pilgrims."

"Dear me!"

"'Tis merely because of the Saint Alba's pilgrim being on *Saint Toole's* day. And then there's the issue of the fire...well, it all began with a bit of friendly rivalry, but now it has become something of an issue."

"Who is Saint Toole? What is *it* all about, exactly?" she enquired.

"What? Has Jack not told you about Saint Toole," Ingrid cried, "our patron saint?" She playfully nudged Jack's shoulder, then slipped her arm around his.

Clara shook her head. "No. He hasn't. What is it all about?"

"Now, Jack, how neglectful you have been!" Ingrid teased, snuggling up to him.

"The subject didn't arise," he replied coolly.

"Let me explain," said Father John. "Godwick started off as a toll bridge, on the best crossing point of the river, which happened to be on a pilgrimage route. That's why Baron Montforte—ancestor of the current Lord de Montfort—built the castle. Then the town grew up around it, and Saint Toole was a scribe at the castle. He also made the most exquisite illuminations for the town, copying many pages of the Bible, and preaching to all. He was a very holy man. They knew even then that his writing was inspired by God. But when some wicked marauders seized him and tried to stop him from proclaiming God's greatness, he simply ignored their orders and continued to write for the glory of God. So before they made a Roman torch of him, they cut off his right hand and stuck it on a pike outside the city walls."

"As a warning," Ingrid interjected.

"Was it the same marauders that attacked Saint Alba?" Clara asked.

"I know not," Father John said with a shrug. "But the point is, Saint Toole's hand did not decay, nor did it rot in any way. It remained in perfect color and condition, impaled on the pike. No crows pecked at it, no maggots crawled within its perfect flesh. And then, of course, came the miracles. His hand was taken down in due course and placed in a reliquary by the local monks, and he was canonized. We have his hand still, as our holy relic. It's in the old church now."

"And on Saint Toole's day, it's paraded through the streets of Godwick, no doubt," Clara said.

"Exactly so! We had a beautifully carved hand as well, made out of olive wood from the Holy Land. But with all the pilgrimages passing through here, a Palmers' Guild was set up..."

"The first and only guild in the town," Jack put in bitterly.

"And they built the new church," Father John said, "a new,

bigger church. I have no quarrel with that, but now the Palmers' Guild and its parish have started supporting the Saint Alba's pilgrimage parade, rather than Saint Toole's parade, which happens to be on the same day. However, I have always been of the opinion that their parade could be moved."

"And their pilgrim's hostel is more like a tavern than a hostelry," Howard grumbled.

"And it has the bathhouse," Mildred snapped. "We seldom see a traveler in here thanks to the cursed Palmers' Guild."

Clara nodded. She and Jack stared into their tankards.

"Yet it is I to whom the people come for weddings and baptisms," Father John bemoaned. "I have three visits to make yet before the bell, and I've had five burials this month, three in one week. That is six widows in my parish to worry about. I've taken on another boy from one of the families, but I can only do so much. It's assistants I need, rather than altar boys. Bishop Remfrey has given his word that he will send me another curate, but I'm still waiting. And I've got this year's Saint Toole's parade to organize. I have a mind to make a big impression this year, which is why I'm so glad to finally have a decent Saint Toole's hand. Last year Saint Alba's had a splendid jaw that opened and shut, which is ludicrous, considering Saint Alba was silent. But the people loved it." Father John paused a while before turning to the joiner. "You were able to make the new hand move, were you not?"

Robert shook his head as the group sighed in commiseration. "Alas, no, Father. But all the fingers are separated."

Clara said, "It is a very fine frame indeed! Jack, I implore you to finish it off!"

Father John nodded vigorously to Jack, but he made no audible reply.

Father John turned back to Clara. "For three years we have tried earnestly to replace our olive hand, but it has proved beyond our means! Each year we have tried a new, alternative one. But, alas! Saint Alba's has been upstaging us in every parade since the fire. If we fail to put on a spectacular show this year, I fear our parade day will become a thing of the past." Here he eyed his flock sternly. "And the holy day along with it."

"Are you saying we would lose a holiday?"

"Never!"

Father John nodded sternly. He turned to Jack. "Jack, I prayed for a solution—upon my knees! It is my strong belief that you have been sent by God to finish Saint Toole's hand."

There was a chorus of “Here! Here!” and raised tankards.

Father John left, and Simon pushed the hand over to Jack. “You will do it for us, will you not, Jack?”

“Of course he will! Surely you will not forsake us, dearest Jack?” Ingrid asked.

He sighed, keeping the company waiting for a moment before replying, “Oh very well! Aye, I’ll do it!”

He placed his hand on the frame and slid it toward his chest.

Chapter Eight

"Look, Clara! Look!" William squeaked as he ran up the stairs, a bundle of off cuts clenched in his fists. His eyes were wide and bright, and his cheeks flushed.

"Mm?" Clara acknowledged the boy absently, eyeing not William, but Dermot.

"Close the shutters! It's too bright, too drafty!" the old man croaked. His face was certainly paler and seemed thinner than usual.

"See what I have!" The boy skidded to a halt at the bedside, shaking the bundle of rags. They were mostly long, thin and a variety of shades of brown, blue and red. "These will be perfect!" he enthused, holding out the rags for Clara to see.

"Mm...that's nice."

William licked his lips and explained, "We could sew them so they dangle out of the bottom of the wrist—just slightly—not too much. They'll look like blood and flesh, newly torn...and this one—the blue one—can be a big vein!"

"Ugh!" Clara frowned and stared down her nose at the scraps. "Have you been to a few executions, then?"

"It will look so real! I can be the one to sew it, Miss Clara. Indeed I *should* be the one for the task, because I can picture it in my mind's eye. Do you know, Miss Clara, I have a mind that I may have received a vision from God."

"Shut up, boy!" Dermot said, "My head aches. Close the blinds, woman!"

William and Clara looked down at the old man.

"He does not seem to be well today," William remarked quietly.

"Indeed not." Clara ushered William downstairs to the shop. "I had to help him onto the chamber pot, and he hardly groped me at all. I am very worried about him. I wonder when Jack will be back?"

William shrugged. "He said he hopes to bargain Mr. Elwood down a little. He took the very last of his money to get cloth for the orders."

"Mm...there won't be anything to pay a physician, then." She took hold of William's elbow, moving him to descend the stairs before her, and confided in him as they entered the shop, "I was thinking Dermot may need some letting."

Clara moved to the doorway and stared out into the street, and William began to lay out his material scraps.

"Miss Clara, do you think Master Jack will let me help with the hand for Saint Toole's parade?" he asked after some time.

"I cannot see why not. Indeed, I imagine he will be glad of the help. Then he can pursue more profitable work." Clara took out her comb and used it to scratch at her scalp. "Saints alive, I itch all over! 'Tis that old man. Every time I tend to him, I can feel the vermin crawling onto me, seeking out a new home. I itch for hours afterwards."

"What if it is his wickedness that gets beneath your skin?" William suggested.

Clara gave him a startled look. "I fancy he is merely riddled with vermin. I wonder if we could get him down to the baths?"

The boy twiddled with his treasured material scraps, arranging them in a gory display of tendrils. "He is banned from the baths," he said idly.

"Indeed?"

"Yes, miss! He grabbed a serv..."

"Spare me the details! Well, how about this scheme; if the water carriers come by, I shall buy some water and we can boil it up and all have a good wash tonight. I purchased some of Mother Huckle's concoction from the market. I am told it is a wondrous cure for ailments such as these."

"But the lice will come back again."

"No they will not. I propose to wash Dermot as well. That will drive the little devils out!"

Clara moved to the door and peered down the street. "I think Dermot needs new bedding, too. I suspect he pees in his bed....oh, there goes Ingrid! Hark at her beautiful braids! They shine like spun gold—how dare she look so lovely!" But Clara smiled warmly as she spoke and waved to her. "I wonder where she is going so beautifully dressed up? I wager she's on her way here to charm our Jack into her bed!"

"Mayhap she's going to see Sir Burk de Montfort," William suggested.

Clara shot him a hopeful look and crossed to his side. "Burke? Why do you say that?"

He never got to answer, as Ingrid, with a charming smile and the scent of roses clinging to her person, stepped in through the door. The bell above it announced her arrival with a tinkle. Ingrid approached Clara and gave her a warm, guilt-inducing hug.

"How are you, dear Clara? I would not have come in but I saw you at the door, beckoning, and I thought—I hoped—Jack may have already finished my new sleeves?"

"No. But it's ready for a fitting. Would you like to try it on?"

"Are you sure William can do that much?" Ingrid eyed the boy dubiously. He was still busy playing with his bundle of off cuts.

"I can," Clara said confidently, "I know the business very well. My father is a tailor."

"Will Jack not consider such a move interfering? Mayhap he returns to find you've measured me and decided on the length?"

"Who knows how long he'll be?" Clara hurried to fetch the almost completed work and thrust it in Ingrid's hands. "Go on, try it on! Jack's gone to market to buy some woolen cloth."

Ingrid let her mark the hem but fussed all the while, and when the fitting was done she seemed doubtful of the accuracy of her measurements.

"I'll linger here a moment longer to see if Jack returns, for he may wish to make sure of the length. Besides, there is no hurry; I believe he will have it sewn in plenty of time for the Saint Toole's parade...I'm freezing after all this undressing, allow me to warm myself before I go," she finished and made herself comfortable by the fire.

Clara felt obliged to stay downstairs with their customer. She fussed about, tidying up, darning in the "proposed hem" her hands itched to sew in properly. Of course it was the right length! How many lengths could there possibly be? Ingrid was merely delaying—hoping to see Jack. Why, she could have sewn her own sleeves, surely! Clara swept the already clean floor and tidied the work bench once again.

"William," she said, "did Jack not set you some work? No darning, nor hemming? A buttonhole to sew, perhaps?"

"I had to sweep and clean up, and then as soon as Ingrid's sleeves are measured, I am to begin the hem," he replied.

"Well, there you are, Ingrid! William should sew them at once. We cannot have the apprentice lying about the shop, twiddling his thumbs, arranging off cuts into innards..."

"What is it you are doing there, William?" Ingrid asked, frowning at his arrangement of rags.

He told her of his plan for the hand, and she thought it was a fine idea. She left the fire and came over to his display.

"Splendid! Oh, it will look perfect! Get the hand out and let us see!" Ingrid said. She and William laid the hand out on the workbench, sweeping aside Clara's neat arrangement of Jack's tools to make space. Together they crowded over the frame, draping off cuts here and winding off cuts there, and making earnest plans.

Clara watching the pair dubiously. "Will Jack not find *that* interfering?" she muttered. But they ignored her—or else they were too engrossed to hear.

However, Clara noticed with some irritation, they heard Dermot's loud groaning from upstairs clearly enough.

"Is that Dermot?" Ingrid asked, looking upward, the gory display flopping to the bench.

"Yes it is," Clara replied curtly.

"He sounds dreadful! Are you sure he's quite well?"

"He complains of a headache."

"Indeed?" Ingrid moved to the bottom of the staircase. "It sounds as though he is dying. Whatever have you been doing to him?"

"I beg your pardon? Why, nothing!" Clara spluttered, "Nothing at all! I've been very attentive...as for deliberately harming..."

"Clara!" came Dermot's haunting wails from upstairs, "Do not forsake me; why have you abandoned me?"

"Oh!"

"The poor old dear," Ingrid said reproachfully.

"He is not a poor old dear! I do my best for him," Clara snapped, and cried up the stairs, "Dermot, I have *not* abandoned you!"

A pitiful groan drifted down to the shop.

"I tell you, 'tis merely a headache!"

Ingrid raised her eyebrows. "*Merely* a headache?"

"Well, what would you have me do?" Clara asked. "We have no money for calling a physician..."

"Lord no! All they do is peer at flasks of pee and prod and poke," Ingrid said, and, hitching up her skirts, she began to climb the stairs. "I am certain between the two of us—a novice and a woman of the world—we can procure a cure for him. No, fear not, Clara; I am all too familiar with his roving hands."

Clara sighed heavily. "And talking of hands, William, put that Saint Toole's one away now. Let us go up and make Dermot comfortable!"

And they followed Ingrid to the old man's bedside, where she stood, frowning down at him. She covered her mouth and nose with her hand. Clara stood by her and they spoke in whispers.

"Hark! I have been trying to clear the smell away since I arrived. But it always returns," Clara said.

"It may be the cause of his headache."

"Ah, but methinks he is the cause of the smell."

"He has had that headache before. A few times," William said.

"Indeed? What does he do for it?" Ingrid asked.

The boy shrugged. "I know not. He rolls about in bed and complains."

"Did he ever hire a physician? What did they do?"

"They said they would have to drill a hole in his skull to cure him. So he kicked them out and got better on his own."

Ingrid coughed.

"Mm...indeed," Clara muttered dryly.

"He says he needs to be purged from his sins. Cleansed and set free from all his guilt," William embellished, his voice rising.

"Hush! The light burns my eyes!" Dermot complained.

"I do believe we ought to change his bedding...again."

"And bathe him," Ingrid said.

"What? Do you think so too?" Clara began to think that Ingrid may make a good friend, after all.

Ingrid nodded earnestly. She leaned down and spoke to Dermot in clear, slow tones. "We're going to cleans you from your sins, old Dermot."

"I need last rites," he groaned.

"Yes, of course."

Ingrid stood up and consulted Clara. "Hark at that! He had ample opportunity and yet made no effort at all to grope me. It bodes very ill—very ill indeed!"

"Do you think he does need...last rites?"

Ingrid considered for a moment before replying, "A bath first."

"And let us burn his bedding. And his clothes too. He has another smock. I saw it when I was cleaning the house up," Clara said. She eyed the grimy sheets. "But what are we to do with his linen?"

"Boil them. Hang the blanket out to air," Ingrid said decisively. "William, stoke up the fire, and procure two buckets of water. And, William, dear," she said, handing him a coin from her purse, "get some soap from Mother Huckle's stall at the market. No, Clara, I won't hear a single word of protest!"

This annoyed Clara, and embarrassed her. All these things she'd planned over and over in her head. She even had some of that expensive soap herself, but one thing had held her back. Yet there was Ingrid, making her look a fool, going on as if this was all her brainchild! She braced herself to protest and began, "But I..."

Ingrid wasn't listening to her; she waggled her index finger. "No, no! Allow me! Let me give you at least one taste of Mother Huckle's amazing cure for personal vermin. You, my dear friend, shall soon give your entire life to God; I am offering only this one little act of charity. Not another word! Instead, find the biggest empty barrel you can. We shall stand him up in it, and scrub him down, then rinse him with hot water."

Clara voiced that one last, major concern she had about bathing Dermot. "But, should we...I mean, he's a man...naked...and we are—you know—maidens."

"As you witnessed, he has been rendered useless. He made no effort to touch me. Indeed, he hardly noticed that I was a woman at all, and you know what that man is made of. He used to practically chase me around the place, even when he was first taken ill. And for that reason I stopped bringing him broth."

Clara blinked. "Oh. I thought I was the only one."

They soon had the fire roaring dangerously in its grate, a heavy cauldron of water singing as it came to the boil. With the pair working to maximum efficiency and Dermot out of sorts, they had him stripped, damped and scrubbed down before he had his wits about him. As his protests drained from an indignant roar to feeble whimpers, William and Ingrid pinned him down as Clara rubbed the soap into him mercilessly. Over every itching welt, every scabby imperfection.

Maneuvering him into the barrel was the difficult task. After several attempts with their patient flailing and squirming to get loose, they formed a cunning plan. As the cauldron of water began to bubble, they laid the empty barrel down and slid him, prostrate and slippery from the concoction massaged into his skin and hair, into the barrel's cavernous mouth. Only it didn't seem that large once he was in it. Ingrid had him firmly from behind, under the armpits, and William was required to hold the barrel steady.

Poor Clara was in charge of keeping Dermot's middle and legs aimed into the barrel as they hoisted both bath and bather to stand upright. Then, with lightning speed, Clara topped up a half-filled wooden bucket of cold water with the hot water from the cauldron and doused Dermot all over, sponging him with a handful of linen rags. She barely took in that Ingrid had stepped back and removed the apron Clara had lent her for the task. Clara had got her own clothes smeared and doused in the throws of the job.

* * * *

It was at this point that Jack returned to the shop. Hearing Dermot's plaintive wails, he bounded upstairs to find Clara—obviously the guilty one—pouring steaming water over the old man's head and stroking his back as the water cascaded down his naked form. William was stirring some vile-smelling thing in the cauldron over the fire, and Ingrid—a client for all intents and purposes—stood watching dumbly.

"What in God's name are you doing? You'll drown him! Why is he naked? What is that brew?"

Ingrid uttered a small cry—or was it a giggle?

"I'm trying to rid him of all his mites," Clara said. "We're giving him a bath."

"You look like a witch's coven, in the middle of some evil spell!"

"I think he'll feel a whole lot better after this," Clara said. "Will you not, Dermot?"

The old man groaned and began to shiver.

"Hark, you shall kill him!"

"Then at least he will die clean!"

"How could you—upon the eve of becoming a nun—molest a helpless old man like this?"

Clara wiped a stray strand of hair from her face. Her dress was splotched with dark, wet patches and smeared with the soap. Her breathing was deep and her face flushed. She put her hands on her hips. "Molest? I'm doing him a service!"

"That's exactly what I fear—and all before a customer, a member of the public, a witness!" Jack ran his fingers through his hair.

"Indeed," Clara answered passionately, "a witness to the innocence of my intentions—my *good* intentions."

Ingrid bit her bottom lip. "I swear I will not tell a soul. I only came for my fitting...perhaps we could..." She trailed off and indicated the stairs.

Jack stood for a moment, arms rigid at his side. "Yes, of course!"

As he ushered Ingrid out the door, she whispered as she passed Clara, "I shall speak with him...explain gently..."

* * * *

Clara stood for a long time, staring at the doorway. It was

Dermot's chattering teeth that brought her back to the matter at hand. She fetched a low stool and, although it was too late for modesty, she averted her eyes as she helped him to climb out of the barrel. She supported him as he stood by the fire. When his skin was mostly dry, she sat him down; then she and William wrung out the boiled sheets and set them to dry.

"Go and assist Jack now," she told William as she slipped Dermot's head and arms into his clean smock.

Hauling the still steaming water up to the third floor, she stripped and plunged the soap-smeared garments into it. She stoked up the small fire in the room, and put more water on to boil. Standing naked, she washed her entire outfit. Then she soaped herself down and rinsed off with the fresh water.

"There, I feel clean now...purged." Clara pulled her chemise over her head. But she did not feel as satisfied as she ought to. For one thing, the scent of roses did not cling to her.

Chapter Nine

It was a sense of irritation that clung to Clara, actually. She ran with it—used it to bully first William and then Jack into washing down with that Madame Huckle's concoction. It was, after all, Saturday. A good day for a household to clean up. Even Jack had to agree that it was less scandalous, less perverted, if they all took a good scrubbing than if she had attacked a defenseless, dying old man by stripping and lathering him down.

Clara removed her clean sleeves to aid William and to wash their clothes, vigorously. Why did Jack comply, instead of giving her a backhand for her cheek? Because, she told herself righteously, he itched and flaked every bit as much as she did. Because he couldn't deny that the upstairs rooms already smelled fresher. Because she was right to have bathed Dermot.

Jack growled at the expense of Clara's Great Clean Up, and Clara snapped at the filth that had driven her to it. William and Dermot made silent, sheepish eyes at them, but they ignored those plaintive appeals for peace. They bickered all the way, over every little detail they could find to disagree upon.

At last, scrubbed up and squabbled out, they ate supper, Jack and Clara silently gnawing cold pork pie and glaring at each other. Then Jack, grabbing a pipkin, flounced off to the tavern—no doubt to cry on Howard's shoulder!—and Clara went early to bed.

Although they prepared for Mass the following morning in relative silence, the tension had dropped down. The mood in the house was no longer as prickly as wool; it was more like the fuzzy feeling of soft flannel.

Clara took the firedogs from the hearth and scrapped away the ashes. As soon as she heard Dermot stir, she hurried to his bedside to offer to help him use the chamber pot. The room smelled relatively clean, still, considering the shutters had been closed all night, and she wanted to keep it that way for as long as possible. Dermot seemed as bright eyed as ever, his blue eyes sparkling against his ruddy skin.

He beckoned to Clara. "You have rejuvenated me, my darling. Listen carefully..." He beckoned again, waiting until her face was close to his. "You are a beautiful woman."

"Ah, thank you, Dermot. You seem much improved this morning."

"You like to fornicate?"

Clara froze.

Dermot grabbed one of her wrists. "You and me. We could do it, yes?"

Still Clara did not move.

"You do know what fornication is, don't you?"

Clara blinked. "Of course...but. No! You cannot... No!"

Jack, just coming down from the loft room, stood in the doorway. Dermot let go of Clara's wrist as though he'd been bitten.

"I'll help Dermot onto the chamber pot, Clara!" Jack said.

"Yes. Thank you." Clara frowned as she stepped aside. She crossed to the window and wiped her hands.

Dermot slapped at Jack. "Leave me alone! I can do it myself!"

The old man stayed in bed as the other three set off to attend Mass. The church was cold and smelled strongly of polished wood and the dusty air of mason work, as well as the rasping sandalwood tones of incense. Its own strong scent was a good thing; it served to mask the pungent smell of some of the parishioners, as they huddled together in the nave. Only the fullers seemed to have breathing space around them. Clara was glad to have to squeeze up between Jack and William, if only for the body warmth. They were not particularly early getting to the church, and, aside from the crowd in front of them, their view of the altar was obstructed by large pillars, as well as the rood screen. But Clara could make out Father John behind the carved latticework. Her eyes followed the patterns, and she tried to hold a picture of them in her mind. How lovely they would look as embroidery. Dark thread on cream linen, with touches of gold, to echo the candle flames and decorations in the chancel.

Clara drew her attention back to the Mass. She was, after all, going to be a nun soon. But she did not understand much Latin and, with the proceedings hidden behind the screen and pillars, she found it exceedingly hard to concentrate. Around her the congregation fidgeted and jostled. Mothers' attention was taken up with their children, and friends and families chatted and argued. Was that Ingrid, sidling up behind them? A burly smith moved just so that she couldn't see behind him. And, chiding herself for being so fancily distracted, Clara turned back to face the chancel. She had given herself up to God; she should be able to focus on Mass now, feel some difference within her. Mass should mean something now. Perhaps, she decided, this was why nuns and monks were cloistered away—so they could enjoy undisrupted communion with God. This conclusion brought her no peace; only the irritated realization that her mind had been wandering again. And again! She stared hard at Father John's back through the lattice screen...or *was* it Father John saying Mass? Yes, it had to be, surely.

With an exasperated sigh, she gave up trying to concentrate and looked about her. Her eyes fell on Jack, just as he looked her way. A jolt of shock shot through her as their eyes locked. Jack gave her a gentle smile, "I'm sorry about last night...I should never have become so angry over nothing."

She placed her hand over his. "I'm sorry too, for my part. We shouldn't fight. Soon..." She wanted to say, *I'll be gone. We won't see each other ever again*, but the words wouldn't form on her tongue. At that moment—their gazes still fixed on one another—Father John's words filtered through to them.

"Let us offer each other the sign of peace," he said in Latin. But they knew that cue well. Whilst all around them, people moved to embrace and say, "*Peace be with you!*" slowly, they drew nearer. His lips brushed her cheek; she felt the hint of prickle against her skin, felt his strong hands on her shoulders, turned her head towards him slightly so that her lips could meet his. "Peace be with you..."

But in one violent instant, Jack was gone. He was yanked back so suddenly, he fell into his assailant's grasp, leaving Clara's arms flaying as she tried to stop herself from falling on her face.

It was Ingrid! Having crept up next to them, she had grabbed Jack in one determined motion and locked her lips on his. Clara stared in horror. Her heart froze still, her armpits prickled. Jack and Ingrid were kissing! As Clara turned away from the scene, she was vaguely aware of seeing William nudging Jack fiercely, saying, "Peace be with you, Master Jack!"

Someone tugged at Clara's arm, "Peace be with you....peace be with you..."

"A *sign* of peace...just a *sign!*" Father John yelled in English above the hubbub and bustle. Ingrid and Jack were not the only couple who were taking the gesture over the top, and giggles rippled through the congregation. Father John huffed and continued with the Mass. Ingrid, having managed to untangle herself from Jack's grasp, grinned impishly at Clara and mouthed, "Peace!"

Yes, somehow we ran out of time, Clara thought bitterly, underneath a thin crust of a smile.

The congregation lingered outside the church after Mass despite the prickly drizzle. Clara made a point of shaking Father John's hand.

"How is Dermot?" he asked.

"He had a bad spell, but he is much better now, thank you. I almost called for you."

"Was that before or after the dunking?"

Clara blinked. "The what?"

Father John leaned a little closer. "I hear you gave the old devil a dunking in a vat of wine."

"Father! That's not true. Well...I gave him a bath, in a little barrel, if that's what you mean."

Father John rocked on his heels and laughed. "Ah! Rumor has it that you tried to drown him in a vat, for all his lechery."

"I most certainly did not! It was to cleanse him from...no, I meant to help him feel more comfortable...physically..." Clara ran her tongue over the roof of her mouth.

"So, Jack exaggerated a little, did he? Overreacted, did he?"

Clara glanced around. She noticed a few groups of men and women in little huddles. They seemed to be looking at her frequently as they spoke amongst themselves. "Surely these people do not believe that I...do they?"

Father John chuckled and patted her hand. "Have no fear, my child," he said. "You are a lovely girl, and I'm sure the town will accept you. Hark, here comes Ingrid... Ingrid, introduce Clara to a few people, so that she can feel more at home!" Father John turned his attention to Jack, "Jack! Jack, how's the hand coming on?"

Ingrid introduced Clara, to be sure, but said to every person she presented her to, "Clara is going to join the convent of Saint Alba's Jawbone...she's following the pilgrimage...," and they seemed to put up shutters at those very words. They smiled coolly and said how nice, and how was Old Dermot after she'd ducked him in the vat? Was he making a complete recovery?

"Do not forget," Father John cried, as the congregation dispersed into the streets, "Archery practice today! On the common! Compulsory Archery Practice!"

* * * *

Lord de Montfort's soldiers were putting up the row of wicker targets. The lord himself came riding down from his castle on his steed, bringing along his entourage of officers and his wife and her ladies-in-waiting, as well as his nephew, the Sheriff Burke de Montfort. The rest of the gathered people were on foot.

All tradesmen and youngsters had to keep their battle skills honed. Just in case, one day, their town came under siege. His soldiers practiced daily in the castle grounds, of course. But the laymen gathered weekly. First they watched how it should be done as his archers shot volleys of arrows at the targets.

In clear weather and in the summer, the young women came too and stood around in little groups, fluttering their eyelids and helping the men to try that little bit harder. Most of the unmarried young men competed keenly for the maidens' favors, and the older men tried to put the youngsters to shame. Many wives came to watch their sons and husbands too. They sat in huddles, cheering and jeering, breast-feeding their babies and making rude jokes to embarrass the men. The smaller children played around, getting underfoot, and at least once a year someone or other had some sort of accident involving an arrow. Up on the walls, more soldiers lingered in their watch to gaze down lazily at the gathering citizens. They laughed at the bad shots, raised their eyebrows at the good ones and placed bets on who would do best.

* * * *

Clara initially stayed behind while Jack took William to the archery practice. She made a fuss of Dermot over dinner, cutting his meat for him and feeding him. He grinned and patted her thigh, saying, "You're a good woman... Isn't she a good woman, Jack?"

"Mm..."

"No I'm not! I'm merely trying to atone for drowning you in that vat!" She stared pointedly at Jack, who stared out of the window, and Dermot took advantage of their distraction. He asked Clara to help him back into his bed just as Jack and William were leaving for the practice.

"Listen carefully! I have a little secret..." he said as the front door slammed.

Clara bent closer.

Dermot grabbed her hand. "Come, girl, let us get mating."

"What? You wish to go to Matins? I suppose I could accompany you—"

Dermot nodded excitedly. "Aye! Yes! You and me."

"Do you like to attend Matins?"

"Oh, yes, I like it!"

"Well, I could go with you—what time in the morning?" Clara leaned away from Dermot to stop him from stroking her arm. But he had her fast.

"Now, now! Get under the covers with me!"

"What?"

"Before the boys get back. We have time, yes?"

Clara began prying her arm from Dermot's grip. "I think we misunderstood each other."

"Do not be afraid. I have secrets; I know well how to pleasure a woman."

"I beg you, let me go!"

"All women who have known me see what delights are to be had by fornication with me. What is it that troubles you—have you never had a man inside you?"

"No! Never! I am soon to be a novice, remember?" Clara tried to loosen his bony fingers, but in vain; they just kept folding themselves round her sleeves.

Downstairs the doorbell tinkled.

"Thank God! We have customers."

"You should try copulation before you go..."

"The door...someone's at the door," she said, her voice rising, "I'm coming...wait—do not go, I beg of you, I'm coming down! Dermot, *please*!"

"Aye, it's a bad time now," he said, "but give me a kiss, eh? Quickly..." He puckered up.

"Yoo...hoo!" a familiar voice called from the shop.

"Ingrid! Hello! Come on up! *Do* come on up!"

The old man let her go with a sigh and a wink as Ingrid's footsteps drew near. Clara all but flew into her arms, almost knocking her down the stairs.

She smelled of roses again, and her lips were stained with berries and flowers were woven into her plaits. She took Clara's hands in hers and gave them a tender squeeze.

"What ails you, Clara?" she asked. "You appear agitated." Although Clara whispered a hasty reply, Ingrid did not heed it; her focus was on the room. She scanned it quickly and shrugged.

"I think we ought to follow Jack to the practice. That is where he's gone, is it not?"

"Aye! Him and William together."

"Come with me, Clara. We all go to watch the men at their exercise in Godwick. It's great fun."

"We used to couple on the grass, afterwards," Dermot said sleepily, "when the stars came out. It is very good out in the open air..."

"But now you need to sleep, and Clara needs to take a brisk walk."

"Away from him," Clara whispered, as she and Ingrid backed out of the door.

Ingrid linked arms with her, and they hurried out into the streets.

"I'm sure he means no harm," Clara said as soon as she was a safe distance from the house. "He is old and weak headed. And surely he would never...would he? He is old and needs our compassion and understanding. His mind is unclear, don't you think?"

"You are too kind and gentle, my dear Clara. A swift knee to the groin would soon clear his mind."

"*Ingrid!*"

But once again, Ingrid's attention was elsewhere. They had reached the common ground. Her eyes scanned the crowds quickly. "Where's Jack? I can't see him or William."

"There's quite a crowd, considering the small size of Godwick."

"I told you, my dear friend, that archery days are much appreciated here. Afterwards there's cock fighting and sometimes bear bating. Hark!" she whispered in Clara's ear, "There's Burke! Lord de Montforte's nephew. He is the best shot. It is a pity you missed his fine display."

Burke, sitting astride a fighting horse, spotted the girls at once and cantered over. He dismounted and took first Ingrid's hand and then Clara's, kissing each in turn. He met their eyes steadily and murmured his greeting in French. Clara found herself curtseying and fluttering her eyelashes. Then she felt a pang of guilt and glanced around frantically.

Ingrid laughed. "You may as well enjoy a bit of courting while you still can. Our dear Clara, Burke, is shortly to become a novice!" she explained cheerfully, "Indeed, she shall join the Saint Alba's parade. Clara, as you follow the parade, you will be walking behind the richest and noblest families in town, including Lord de Montforte's. Not that you're looking to find a good husband, or enter into society."

"No, quite the opposite."

"Nevertheless, you will be a special member in the parade.

Burke, will you be joining in the Saint Alba pilgrimage this year, or the Saint Toole's parade? I must warn you, Clara, Burke is a terrible flirt when it comes to politics."

"Neither," Burke said. "My uncle, Lord de Montforte, wants his soldiers to keep a high profile and to remain neutral. Last year," he explained to Clara, "there was almost a riot between the two sides. Lord de Montforte is a member of the Palmers' Guild, and so supports the Saint Alba's parade—which is a much better affair, by far. After the pilgrims have gone through town, the guild holds a splendid party at the castle. I am always invited to attend it, naturally. It's a pity you won't be able to go, Clara, as you'll be off to start your wonderful new life as a nun.

"Unless," Burke continued, taking Clara's hand again, "you can be persuaded to change your mind, and stay. Consider, perhaps, becoming...er...I don't know...someone's lover?" He kissed her hand again, his lips lingering on her skin as his eyes held hers. She gaped, shut her mouth, felt a hot flush race across her cheeks.

"As my usual partner has informed me she has no intention of attending the Saint Alba's party, I'll be happy to escort you there... if, that is, you decide to not waste such ... beauty...by cloistering it away."

There was a long silence. At last Burke let her hand go.

"Now, if you'll excuse me, ladies, I have duties to attend to." And with swift gracefulness, he departed.

"Ignore him—he speaks thus to all the girls," Ingrid said flatly.

Clara stared at her shaking hands. "I think I need to sit down."

"He is not even Lord de Montforte's nephew, proper," Ingrid said, glaring after Burke. "His father is the bastard son of some commoner and a disgraced aunt of Lord de Montforte. The highest status he will ever attain is what he is—the Sheriff of Godwick, a soldier of rank in his uncle's army. If he could seriously marry into high society, would he give the likes of you and I the time of day? I think not."

"Yes, yes of course," Clara assured her. "He's merely charming."

"He is a bastard seeking to attain rank, a bombastic cockerel! I loathe him!"

"I gave little heed to his careless words."

Ingrid turned her face slowly to look at Clara properly. Her chest was heaving, her eyes dark and intense. Her expression, however, softened as she met Clara's eyes and a familiar, mischievous grin spread out over face. She took Clara's hand and squeezed it.

"You are truly a wise, good person. And the way you take care of that dirty old Dermot is remarkable. I have no doubt you'll make an excellent nun."

Clara had doubts. In fact, her head swirled with doubts. Big, murky, dark blobs that refused to form into proper thoughts. Things she thought she'd heard, but couldn't quite remember. Things that didn't seem to add up, that didn't feel right. The only clear idea, solid enough for her to hold on to, was that nothing was clear. It sent alarm bells clanging furiously. It made her head ache.

Ingrid, however, seemed to grow almost frantic. She skipped and danced her way across the common, drawing attention from men and flirting shamelessly with them. Jokes poured freely from her lips, and she giggled and hooted at the men, nudging Clara to make sure she laughed too, as a horseman might spur on his sluggish steed. She called out to everyone she knew; hailed this person over there, and introduced that person here to Clara. She instigated a piggyback race among the young—and not so young—couples, by first daring Matilda and Howard to race another couple. Then there was a re-run as more people joined in.

"Who'll ride Jack! Jack needs a partner!" Ingrid cried just as the next race took off. "Clara?"

Even as she proposed it, she jumped on Jack's back.

Clara stood and smiled and watched as wives and girlfriends bumped along on the backs of their jogging partners. The crowds roared with laughter. The beat of galloping hooves drummed in time to her throbbing temples, as Burke and two accompanying officers rode over to disperse the nonsense.

Clara heard him muttering, "Villainous fools!" as he veered his horse round. He looked down at her and said, "It pleases me to see someone knows how to conduct herself properly." And he smiled and winked. Clara thought she could hear Ingrid guffaw, or was it a horse whinnying?

"I have a mind to go home," she said to no one in particular, turning away. The castle walls loomed up beside her as she plodded up the sloping grass toward the market area. Burke was beside her still, on his mount.

He offered her his hand. "I shall escort you; ride back with me!"

"Oh, God, no!" Clara cried. She thought fast and continued, "My head aches; the motion will surely split it apart."

He nodded, his horse pawing the ground as he let her go on her way. He watched her. "Consider my offer!" he yelled after her. She waved briefly and continued homeward.

"Why am I not blinded by his flattery? Why am I not swept off my feet?" Clara scolded herself. "Oh, that I could lose all my powers of reason in a fit of infatuation and run off with this stallion, this wicked tempter! This one chance of avoiding my cursed fate!" She stopped and stood still for a moment. "Of course, if he is my only chance of staying here, living close to...or would it be too painful to bear watching him nesting with that twittering magpie...? Or never to see him again? Which would be the worst evil?"

It seemed Clara was bound to consider Burke's proposal most thoroughly.

Chapter Ten

The next day dawned brilliantly bright and clear, with the sky stretching above the land in a flawless blue. And the sun pledged to blaze down with a Mediterranean strength. Even at dawn, it spread its glowing fingers across town and countryside in a loving caress. And the gentlest of breezes lifted the bird song heavenward. It was a day so beautiful and full of promise that it had to mark something; it could not come along without some significant event.

Clara threw open the shutters and declared, "Oh, what a perfect drying day it is!" Outwardly, at least, she had recovered from yesterday's strain.

"Excellent light!" Jack agreed, tumbling out of his bed. "Rise up William; let us get as much sewing done today as we can. By the way, Clara, did you not follow us down to the practice yesterday? I did not see you there?"

"I was there for a short while. Did Ingrid not tell you? I saw you give her a piggyback."

Jack seemed too involved in buttoning his jerkin to answer. And Clara quickly forced her mind to focus on the washing dilemma.

"I wonder if I should wash the linen?" she pondered aloud. "It would be a shame to waste such a lovely day."

"You've washed everything in sight already!" Jack said. "Indeed, it would surprise me if you have any soap left!"

"But we might not have such good weather again for many a day!" Clara hurried down to open the middle floor windows and rustle up some breakfast. In the end, she decided to take the linen and hang it out of the window for a good airing. And she got Jack to help her get Dermot down the stairs.

"Come on, old man," she said, pushing a low stool against the wall outside the shop. "Jack shall sit you down just here by the door. Is this not a heavenly day?"

Dermot beckoned her closer, muttering, "I must tell you something," but when she bent down he only asked her, "Did you lie down with any man yesterday, on the field?"

"No...um...for pity's sake, Dermot!" Clara shook her head stepped back, but he reached out for her, almost toppling off the stool. And like a fool, she leaned forward instinctively to set him securely in his seat.

Now he had her by her wrist. "Why do you blush? Do you consider yourself above all other women?" He dropped her hand as though it were filth.

Stung at this sudden and unexpected disapproval, Clara said, "Why, no! I do not mean to...have I been self-righteous?"

Dermot considered for a moment, staring ahead dismally. He sniffed gently, and Clara noticed the droop of his mouth with a pang of guilt. She touched his shoulder.

"If my manner is disrespectful...perhaps my father was right to..."

"God put us here, on His green earth, together," Dermot said. "And can you tell me for what purpose?"

"To live...to care for all His creatures..."

"Man on his own could well have cared for the earth, and all its creatures. Why are we here *together?*"

Clara frowned. "So woman can help man?"

Dermot smiled. He turned to face her and beckoned her to come nearer. "I'll tell you."

Clara bent closer to hear his whispered words of wisdom above the growing hub of the streets.

"We are here to fuck!" Dermot said triumphantly. Clara jumped back, but he had her by the wrist again. The same wrist, she noted, with a scowl. What a fool she was!

Despite her anger, her heart drummed like that of a cornered mouse. "Er...surely..." she began in muted tones.

Dermot cut her off. "Without procreation, we would die out, and who would care for God's little creatures then? Eh? That is why it is so good—why it feels heavenly. Because it is heavenly for man and woman to lie together." His own voice, despite its pronounced slur, was fluid and strong.

"I see your point, but...er...surely....?" Clara gave up trying to argue; instead she concentrated on releasing his grip on her. A pair of passing soldiers, turned back to look at the scene, laughed as they continued on their way.

Dermot whispered into Clara's burning ear, "I know how to pleasure a woman. I will kiss every part of you. If you allow me inside, you will open up to me like a flower!"

"Sir! I beg you, stop talking to me in this manner," Clara said, aware of yet more staring pedestrians.

"*Dermot*!" Jack said, leaning outwards from the open shelf, "Behave yourself!"

Clara took full advantage of the distraction, pulling free of Dermot's grip and ignoring his plaintive whine as she fled upstairs. There she hid behind a few hours of domestic chores.

* * * *

Jack came outside, measuring the last few yards of a length of woolen fabric. Pausing as he drew the cloth from the tip of his nose to the length of his arm, he glared down at Dermot. "What have you been suggesting? What are you about? Why do you try to force your attentions on every woman you meet? You must know you will be refused!"

Dermot eyed Jack with equal ferocity. "And you, journeyman, must know your position in this house, and yet you scold me thus!" He turned away, hunching his shoulders against the fresh morning air, and continued, "Besides, I don't know, until I have asked. I am willing to take my chances and be rejected. Indeed, to be rejected is sad, but to yield for fear of rejection is cowardly."

"If you must throw yourself upon women, could you not at least show some decency, and offer a proper marriage proposal?"

"I have no wish to marry her. I merely intend to bed the girl."

Forgetting his careful measuring, Jack furiously scrunched the cloth up into a bundle, all but thrusting it at Dermot, as he leaned in on the old man. "You lecherous villain!"

Dermot flinched visibly, but he was not frightened into silence. "*You* offer her your hand if you are such a noble hero, if you feel she is worth such a commitment!"

Jack gripped the cloth as though it were Dermot's neck in his hands. "She is certainly worth it. But with what do I keep her? All my money has gone into cleaning up your squalor and helping with this ridiculous Saint Toole's venture. Once I have completed the hand, I will surely be thrown out with nothing but my skills! And I must begin again as the day I left my apprenticeship. Clara is the daughter of a prosperous merchant; how will I keep her, old man, you tell me that?"

"Quit badgering me!" Dermot growled. "You are not to use such tones on me. I am your elder, I am your master—and you are my servant!"

"I tell you this as one man to another," Jack said through

gritted teeth, "Leave Clara be!"

He stalked back into the shop, giving the cloth a furious shake before beginning to measure it again indoors.

He cut out an entire order and settled down to sew it before another word was spoken. The shelf opened out onto the street, doubling the depth of the workbench and providing more light to work by. It also enabled Jack to direct an angry glance, from time to time, at the back of Dermot's fuzzy old head outside the shop. At last William, sitting cross-legged on the workbench, broke the silence as he snipped his thread of cotton.

"What a splendid day! I feel like celebrating," he said, looking happily out at the bustling street. "I hope Saint Toole's day is as sunny as this!"

"If you get your work done neatly and in time, you can go out for a bit of play when the sun gets lower," Jack said, his voice restored to its usual gentleness.

Later, Clara peered down the window to ascertain how drowsy Dermot was. Looking down on the top of his head, she could tell by the way it drooped that he had dozed off.

"Poor thing!" she mused. "He has tired himself out, ogling all the women." She had seen some of his old friends stop for a little chat and couldn't help wondering if he had kept to the same subject he seemed so obsessed with when he spoke to her. By the hurried and flustered departure of some of them, it was obvious that he tried his luck at every opportunity.

Taking a basket and a pipkin, she went down the newly scrubbed stairs. Jack and William were still seated on the workbench, sewing in silence.

"I shall go and buy some meat to cook with the beans tonight; is there anything else you need?" she said quietly to Jack.

Jack glanced outside before replying, "Aye, he's asleep now—you can pass him in safety."

Clara gave him a sheepish grin as she made for the door.

"Clara!" Jack called. Dermot twitched in his sleep, and Clara eyed him nervously, before looking at Jack. But all Jack said was, "I'm...er...I'm sorry, that..."

He left the sentence hanging, and Clara shrugged good-naturedly. "He means no harm, and no harm has been done!"

But of course, she hadn't gone far when she fell into a deep wondering. She was reminded of Burke, saying, "Think about it!"

Had Burke meant marriage? Because if he had, simply living her days out within sight of Jack may be a better life than her other option. Or was she imagining a deeper meaning to each remark? Was Jack sorry that she had to put up with Dermot's lechery, or was he really saying that he was sorry he did not—could not—return her feelings? Or was he sorry that she was going to be a nun? Did he return her feelings without knowing how she felt?

Clara stopped so suddenly that a man from behind bumped into her. She barely heard or acknowledged his mumbled apology. *Return her feelings?* Did she want to be a nun? If she truly could, would she choose a life of sin and disobedience? Should she take Burke up on his offer? Was that a proper offer, though? She groaned and put her hands to her forehead. Where could she find some wise council?

"Father!" Clara called, running into the cool, dim sanctuary of the church. Her cries bounced off the stone walls and vaulted ceilings. "Father John! Oh, where is Father John?"

A few scattered parishioners looked up from their own meditations. Although this was only a church, not a cathedral, its open spaces nevertheless seemed immense, and belittled all people seeking sanctuary within its thick walls. Shortly, a thin curate appeared from behind a stone pillar to quiet her. He listened to her pleas, then hurried off to fetch Father John.

When the priest came, his footsteps echoing an announcement of his arrival, Clara rushed to him and took his hands in her clammy ones.

"Oh, Father," she said, "I need to make a confession. I need to talk. I've had these truly awful thoughts. Powerful thoughts, about living in sin...not becoming a novice. And I don't know what Jack means, or what Burke means, yet I think I know, and when I think that, then I believe I am hoping rather than knowing although I am certain of what Dermot means, and I know not if I should be so tolerant towards him. Only I feel sorry for him, he's old and feeble in the head, and there's this cradle up in the loft room. But he's not my main concern. It's Jack! No, it's not! It can't be. It should not be so...but it is."

"My dear child," Father John frowned, "are you making a confession now? Then let's go into the confessional."

"Now, then," he said, when they knelt in their little spaces, hidden from each other's face by a lattice screen. "Have you sinned?"

"Yes. In thought. I thought, 'I don't want to be a nun.'" And she told him about her offer from Burke.

"Do you want to stay and be his lover, hopefully to be his wife one day?" Father John asked.

"No. I think not. Surely not? I do not know."

"Well, think very carefully, before you give up one clear, certain path for an obscure promise. Many men dangle marriage in front of a woman, in order to extract...er...other favors from her," Father John warned.

"Yes," Clara said, her head clearing slightly, "yes, this is true. I have become used to Dermot being more direct with...that. But what about Jack?"

She told him how he had said he was sorry, but he hadn't said for what. "And I thought he was sorry that Dermot speaks to me with such vulgarity—that he cannot protect me from that. Then I thought, he may have been saying sorry he can't...you know... sorry, but that he cannot love me. Or want me to stay, even only for...that thing that Dermot and now Burke seem to...you know... want. A lot of."

Father John sighed. "Women seem to spend a lot of time wondering just exactly what a man means when he speaks. Men, I'm afraid, don't mean very much at all. The main concern for you to worry about is *your* thoughts, your doubts about going into the convent."

"But I can't not go," Clara whispered. "That would be disobedience to my father. That is also where the sin lies. I see now! I cannot fail go to the convent. No wonder I felt such turmoil; I was undoubtedly in the grasp of the very Devil himself. That is my sin—thinking I will not go into the convent. And Burke was sent to tempt me in the flesh. And Dermot was sent to show me what becomes of a person corrupted by lust—what I could become. I will go to the convent. I will be obedient. I will not think about Jack again. I'm sorry for my sin and any others I have forgotten. And I promise never to sin again."

Father John sighed heavily. "Yes, I suppose you could look at it that way. But if you have any more doubts, or worries about becoming a novice, return at once to me. In the meantime, make an act of contrition..."

And he absolved her and blessed her. She said her prayers and lit two candles; then she tripped out into the blinding light. Pausing on the steps of the church, she breathed in deeply, coughing a little, as the heat of the day had sent the gutter contents into rapid putrefaction. She stepped purposefully out with a sense of peace—brittle though it was, it was still there, and not to be scoffed at. And she reminded herself how this sense of peace draped her shoulders like a gentle cloak after each encounter in her Lord's house. And she was glad to become a nun, just then.

Upon returning to the shop, however, her thoughts were plunged immediately into the earthy realm of the here and now. Dermot, his head lolling in sleep, was drooling, and she felt bad at having told tales of his lechery to the priest. He was, after all, a sad old man, clinging to the one comfort he had known in life.

Clara smiled, thinking what a good nun she was turning into, and bent forward to wipe the spittle from Dermot's chin. His lips were blue. She lifted his head up and saw the purple tinge to the tip of his nose.

"Dermot!" she said, slapping him lightly on his cheeks. Then she slapped him harder. He groaned. "Jack!" she screamed, "Jack, quick! He's not right!"

Jack was out in a flash. They heaved Dermot up, each supporting him under an arm, and dragged him indoors and up the stairs.

"William, call a physician," Jack said, pinching Dermot's cheeks and peering at him, "No, fetch Father John! No—both! Fetch a priest and a doctor of sorts, anyone who is available."

* * * *

Father John's feet pounded on the beaten earth street. He held the hem of his habit under one arm, an icon of Saint Joseph, patron saint of departing souls, under the other, and a vial of oil in his grasp. At his side, a little behind him, followed a curate. His effeminate trot was impaired because he was carrying a vessel of holy water, and he was also in charge of the chalice with the communion host in it. And he was trying very hard not to spill a drop of water nor a crumb of host along the way. He could not hold the long skirts of his habit out of the way, but had to be content with brushing them aside with a little sideways kick every fourth step. And worse still, two dogs were in hot pursuit. Each time they came within biting range, the curate extended his kick out at the dogs, almost causing his precious burden to fall to the ground.

People stopped and stared, and two young children joined in the race. For a while, they all had to dodge through a gaggle of geese being led to market. The dogs foolishly turned on the geese and were beaten with a stick by the gooseherd and set upon by the hissing geese. It must have been an act of God, as thereafter, the dogs lost all interest in chasing Father John's entourage. However, Father John had to kick at a rather vicious goose as it nipped his exposed calf, and this motion caused him to stop dead. The curate bumped into him and fell down, holding, by yet more divine intervention, his precious cargo upright and above his head.

As he sprang to his full height again, some holy water did slosh out, anointing the goose and its herder who, full of apologies, swung round with his trusty stick and guided the stray back into the flock.

A nearby beggar followed the drops of spilling water with his keen eye and flung himself prostrate on the earthen road, scratching at the sprinkle of holy water where it fell, and rubbed the muddied drops into his skin, making a sign of the cross on his forehead. He reached out imploringly for another blessing, for more holy water, but got only dust in his eyes for the priest and his assistant, oblivious to his groveling, had hurried on to give Dermot his last rites.

As Father John later said to Clara and Jack, "He either slept through it all, or didn't have the strength to open his eyes. The important thing is that the intention was there. We went through the motions as best we could."

Dermot came to, briefly, twice. Once he opened his eyes as the physician bled him into a little bowl, and he made the doctor and the lingering priest witness formally as he bequeathed his house, his shop and all his other earthly goods to, as he put it, "...to the one who is as a son to me. Once my junior, and companion, and the one who took care of me. Jack. My shop, apprentice, and house must all go to Jack Paisley."

And the second time Dermot stirred, he looked blearily at Clara as she wiped the spittle from the corner of his blue lips. He beckoned her nearer, indicating she should bend over him so that she could hear his weak voice. He grabbed her hand, making his letting wounds bleed afresh, and said, "You are a beauty...I want..."

"Ah! Pray, do not tire yourself apologizing to..."

"I want to rivet you!"

"*Dermot!*" Clara whipped her hand from his, noticing, with a twinge of guilt and pity, that he made no attempt to hold on to her. She shrank back, staring at his limp hands.

"I'll bring William in," she muttered, hurrying from the room.

When William came in to say farewell to his master, Dermot lay very still, with his eyes shut and his face ashen. His breathing grew more and more shallow. William stared at him for a while before being led from the chamber, away from the horrors of death, to continue working on the finer details of the tendrils of the Saint Toole's hand. It looked very good already, thanks to his attention to detail.

Jack spent the night in the solar with Dermot, who appeared to sleep peacefully. But the next morning Dermot was as cold and pale as marble. And Clara and Jack laid him out and washed him together.

"Does he really have no living relatives?" Clara asked, breaking the silence.

"Not even relatives of his late wife. They all died in the plague," Jack said. They crossed themselves and continued working quietly. All that broke their silence was the trickle of water falling into the basin as Clara wrung out the washcloth.

"Did you know her?" she asked at length. "His wife."

"No. She'd died before I came here the first time. I thought at first he was newly widowed—you know how he behaves...behaved with women—but his wife had passed on about five years then already. Apparently she died in childbirth."

Clara told Jack about the cradle and baby clothes in the loft room.

"None of their children lived to be so much as a year old," Jack said. He looked at Dermot and sighed. "Then his wife died giving birth to their final, sixth child—a stillborn. She was too old by then. Forty-something."

"Do you think that made him...the way he was?"

"What? A horny old toad? No! I believe he was always so. When he spoke about his wife once, he told me it was a just punishment for him. He said he had always slept with many other women—soldier's girls, market women from the countryside, whores from the bathhouse, anything in a skirt. He said that his sins rotted the cradle of his wife."

"That is terribly sad," Clara murmured, pulling the shroud over Dermot's face.

"Aye, but it never stopped him. One drunk night of remorseful weeping, and then he would return to his old ways. Forever on the hunt," Jack said, fetching the binding. "'Tis a pity our Good Lord did not see fit to rot his tool in the bargain."

After a shocked silence, Jack begged Clara's pardon. "You have heard enough smut to last you a lifetime already, without me taking on where he left off!" He looked at her ruefully.

"All is forgiven," Clara said, reaching out to him, but her hand was still clammy from the washing. And it had the feel of death on it too. So, no doubt, did Jack's. She quickly drew away and began clearing up, avoiding his eyes. "You meant no harm. Nor did Dermot. And it feels wrong to speak ill of him. Let us say a rosary for him, at least? Father John declared he will bury him very soon, as it is summer and the weather is especially warm this month. He will be laid to rest before Saint Toole's day, Father John said. Saint Toole's parade and the pilgrim march are but a few days away! I cannot believe it is so soon at an end...my visit here. Dermot is gone and I shall be gone too, shortly. How strange that feels!"

It felt awful, really. With a heavy heart, Clara felt the bump on her tongue and hushed her words. Unaware of her frequent sighs, she cleaned and cooked, then picked up her spindle, while Jack and William returned to work downstairs in the shop.

Chapter Eleven

A blanket of mackerel clouds stretched across the horizon as they lowered Dermot into his grave, and the wind tugged at the black veils over the women's faces, teased their dark surcoats and buffeted the men's capes. Jack was quite surprised at the amount of people who had come to bid the old tailor goodbye. He had paid for the little choirboy singing a final tribute at the graveside; his high, thin voice was flung about on the stiff breeze, whipping around their ears like the ghostly cries of a swallow. Apart from the choirboy, and of course, Father John, everyone was there out of choice. And they had the grace to look solemn, sad even, staring desolately at the shrouded figure, as Father John stepped back to allow the bearers to lower Dermot down. It was very early, as early in the morning as the Church would allow, and the day had yet to heat up and, hopefully, clear up. Someone leaned close to him—a woman—he could smell the floral scent on her skin, feel her surcoat whipping against his legs.

It was probably Clara. She had been so glum, blaming herself for having put Dermot in the sun, for having washed him and, amazingly, even for having constantly refused his ludicrous advances. She would be most in need of comfort. Unable to draw his eyes from Dermot, Jack reached out his arm and put it around the damsel's shoulder, soft and rounded, and drooping slightly. And the slightest of smiles played on his lips as her head rested on his chest, ever so lightly. Just a gentle gesture of comfort, between two good, old friends, feeling sad together.

"Poor Jack," she murmured into his hair. And he realized, as a chill ran up his spine, that it was not the voice of Clara. In that same instant, he saw her—Clara—standing to the left of him, with her arm around little William in a similar gesture of comfort, her eyes fixed in hollow desolation upon his own embrace. His heart sank with embarrassment and regret as he realized she was scowling at him, through narrowed eyes. Or was it just the wind causing her to crease her eyes like that? He quickly took his arm from around his supposed companion. But his hurried movement was interpreted all round as simply his taking the cue to be the first, rightfully, to drop a handful of earth into the grave.

As the rest of the congregation turned to line up behind him, one by one, casting their handfuls of clayish soil into the grave, he noticed Burke, of all people, in the huddle. And Burke was glaring at him, in the same way as Clara was. And the woman he had embraced? Ingrid, of course, casting him a lowered smile from behind her mourning veil.

That gentle sorrowfulness one feels at gravesides and other such farewells trickled away into irritation, and Jack jumped, ready to punch out, when someone slapped his back.

"Jack, old boy!" Howard cried, "I beseech you, do not be so downcast. It was a happy release, and we all know how well you treated him. Come, let us meet together, every one of us, after the day's work, to cheer you up!"

"Aye!"

"Sound advice!" the congregation murmured as they picked their way over the sodden graveyard path.

Ingrid whispered into Jack's ear, lingering a moment as she went by. "I'll wait for you at the tavern!" She let her fingers brush lightly across his. Clara, on the other hand, stamped past him with her arms folded, her gaze turned stoically away from him. Jack heaved a sigh and gave Howard a nod and a wave before joining the departing guests as they filed out of the graveyard.

* * * *

That evening all Dermot's old customers and friends came to his house to pay their last respects, including a crowd of faces now growing familiar to Clara. Howard and Matilda, the young joiner with his bodhrán, the neighbors and the tailor Gimmer all came to comfort Jack and William, and to offer one last toast to Dermot's empty place. They each stayed on a little, making a gathering crowd, toasting and toasting again. Father John came to bless the house and lead them in prayer. He stopped in the shop to look at how the parade day hand was coming along, and was delighted with the nearly completed item.

When offered a bit of ale, he accepted and raised his tumbler to Jack, saying, "Ah, a splendid hand you and your apprentice are busy with, Jack." Then he went from guest to guest, describing in great detail how the replica of Saint Toole's hand was coming on.

"That'll show them Saint Alba pilgrims!" someone cried enthusiastically.

Others agreed, and they all had a toast to Saint Toole, and another to Jack's craftsmanship. Cheeks began to flush, while eyes twinkled blearily. The solemn murmuring grew louder and merrier, and when the pipkins were dry, the gathering of friends and neighbors found themselves wandering down to Howard's tavern in unison to refill them. Somehow, they wound up lingering in the tavern to have that one last drink together. They all felt very loving toward each other. Even Clara didn't feel uncomfortable when Ingrid linked her arm in hers; indeed, she felt a warm flush of sisterhood as she raised a toast to Clara.

"You are a truly wonderful nurse," she said, and they each took a swig from their beakers.

"Truly? I thought mayhap it was all my doing," Clara said. "You know, bathing him, sitting him outside..."

Ingrid shook her head. "You tried your best, and because you are such a kindly soul, you feel remorseful sorrow at Dermot's death."

They drank to that. "You contended with that man's feeling fingers and lurid tongue with no complaint—like an angel. You, my friend, are a saint!"

At this Clara smiled gratefully and drank deeply. "Ah, do you truly think so?" she asked.

Ingrid nodded animatedly, "Do you know, I believe you have been directed by God to become a nun. I envy you. I merely flounder hither and thither, with no proper direction in life, vaguely hoping to marry some day. But you—you were made for purer, greater things. It is obviously your destiny to be a bride of Christ."

"Perhaps you're right." Clara sighed and drank very, very deeply.

Ingrid frowned and took her hand. "Is that a trace of doubt I hear in your tone? So often such a choice is forced upon a girl."

Clara glanced about her frantically before she was able to meet Ingrid's gaze. "Why, no. To be sure. It may have been a...strange, roundabout sort of a calling. But I am certain I have been called by Our Lord. No, indeed, I am sure I wish to go. I am committed."

"I salute you! Clara the nun forever!"

Clara forced a smile and drank deeper still, emptying her tankard.

"Oi! Ingrid, your boyfriend's here," the joiner said, giving her a nudge.

Ingrid glanced scornfully over the crowds at the tall, handsome figure of Burke, talking with a couple of Lord de Montforte's men. She shrugged haughtily. "He is no longer my beau!" Then she leaned forward and whispered in Clara's ear, "And thus saying, dearest Clara, if you wish to sample the pleasures of the flesh while you still can, do not allow these rumors that I have a claim on Burke to hinder you."

Clara stopped and stared at her, mute and still.

Ingrid's eyes widened. "Or are you, indeed, considering his... proposal? Do you doubt your decision to become a nun?" Ingrid asked, grinning impishly.

"Pray, do not confuse me further! I believe my mind is set—until I begin to ponder on my fate; then all at once I am in such turmoil."

Ingrid stole a glance at Jack. Then she wrapped her arm around Clara's shoulders in an ivy grip, propelling her toward Burke. "In that case, you are at least undecided, and at worst, despite your insistence, you have been coerced into your vocation. Allow me to save you from your dilemma, Burke did offer you an invitation to the Saint Alba's Banquet, should you decide against joining the pilgrims. Now is the time to get a confirmation from him on that offer. If he is true to his word, then you can take it as word of God that he is your destiny. If he pretends to know nothing of his suggestion, then Saint Alba's is your fate. However, if you have a mind to forgo entering the convent, secure yourself a good position. Strike while the iron is hot! You cannot wish to forgo a life of glorifying God, only to be left homeless and totally alone!"

"I...er..."

"I can tell you, he has a mind to bed you. Even if you are insistent on becoming a nun, a night of passion before taking your vows, before shutting yourself away from all men—where can the harm be in that? And where is a catch as fine as Burke to be found?"

"But I have never..."

Ingrid squeezed Clara's shoulders and whispered, giggling, into her ear, "He is a very skilled, very attentive lover."

Clara squirmed at the touch of a hot breath on her ear and neck. She laughed delightedly as Ingrid turned her head to face in Burke's direction. And he stood a little away from them, as handsome as a stag displaying his mighty antlers on a misty morn.

Clara shrugged. "If this is the direction of the stream, who am I to fight it?"

Ingrid gave her a playful shove. But it was a long walk to Burke's side. As Clara began to weave her way through the revelers, she caught the jarring scent of manly sweat and heard them throw profanities casually into their conversations. Pausing in her stride to negotiate a path around a huddle of the sheriff's men, still with their armor on, she saw how, even with her height, she was dwarfed by their wide shoulders, their hard biceps. She had to stop dead to keep out of the way of a damsel fleeing, albeit playfully, as a knight made a lunge for her. His breastplate was off, his jack was unlaced, and his braies yellowed with sweat.

Clara swallowed and coughed. She shook her head. "What ale-sodden folly would such a liaison be? No—'tis a nun's life for me to be sure!"

But it was too late; Burke had caught her frightened eye. And he was moving toward her.

"Oh, he frightens me, Ingrid," Clara whimpered. But Ingrid, no longer at her side, was wending her way toward the table where Jack sat.

Burke strode toward Clara, reaching her just as the minstrels struck a dancing tune. He bowed and kissed her hand, and as her knees buckled conveniently into a curtsey she failed to notice how his gaze followed Ingrid, slipping away through the crowds.

"Such a lovely flower to lose," he sighed, his lips lingering on Clara's smooth, milk-white hand.

Thank heavens, she thought, she'd rubbed half a pot of salve into it that morning!

"Have this dance with me," he said, "before you cloister yourself away."

Clara found herself going through the motions in time to the minuet ringing through the tavern. But although Burke held her gaze provocatively most of the time, she noticed how often his glances stole to the farther end of the room, to where hers too were drawn. To the trestle table filled with tradesmen from her side of town. Where Ingrid sat with Jack. Her heart sank, probably as low as Burke's seemed to be. Down on the ale-stained, straw-strewn floor, a lost handkerchief lay ruined and muddied. Trampled underneath their dancing feet. And still they twirled, stepped backed and smiled and...suddenly Burke was not dancing, and Clara couldn't either. He held her close to his chest so tightly that she could not get away. Indeed, she could hardly breath. And her heart was pounding.

"This is no good." Burke sighed. "I cannot do it! I cannot put on a pretense any longer." And he buried his head in her slender neck and breathed, "I sorely need your comfort." His lips brushed against her shoulder, sending cold shivers along her skin, "Come outside, away from the din," he whispered.

Clara's eyes opened wide in her otherwise expressionless face. She felt Burke close to her, but she saw Jack and Ingrid talking, their heads close together, across the room from them.

* * * *

"Burke has very kindly offered to watch out for Clara, during the Saint Alba's Jawbone parade," Ingrid said to Jack. She leaned unnecessarily close to him, and her eyelashes were batting. Jack looked up just in time to see Burke and Clara leave the tavern. He had one hand on the small of her back, guiding her out, creeping towards her bottom, the other gently resting on her elbow.

"So I see," he growled, and drained his cup.

Ingrid immediately refilled it, her breast brushing against his arm as she did so, so close did she lean toward him.

"You, of course," she said, "have been given an honorary position in the parade. Right near the reliquary. Did you know you are to hold the new Saint Toole's replica hand? The one you made."

"It's on the small of her back!" Jack gasped.

"What?"

"Burke's hand! It's on Clara's back. Are they going outside?"

Ingrid put her hand on Jack's arm, "Well, they're dancing, aren't they. Look, Clara's promised to devote her life to God. Surely, just days before going into a cloister, she wouldn't..." She let her words trail off and gazed coyly at Jack. Her index finger traced the grain of the wooden table, edging toward his hand.

"She had better not." Jack drained his drink again, his eyes never leaving Clara and Burke.

"Why does she have to be so well behaved?" Ingrid snapped.

"Because she's so...she's so... I can't bear to think of her spoiling all that with...him."

"Well, don't. Think of the parade," Ingrid said soothingly, her fingers edging closer and closer to his hand. "You'll have Saint Toole's severed hand, and she'll be with the pilgrims, as will Burke, so I'll be beside you. We'll go together, you and I, shall we not?"

"Right! That's it! They're leaving," Jack snapped, jumping up and darting into the crowds. "I'm going..."

"Jack! Your drink...! Oh, damnation!" Ingrid slapped the table hard.

* * * *

"No," Clara murmured, "How odd! Suddenly I feel nothing for you. You don't tempt me in the least. No man does." Save one. The one person who could have tempted her away from the protection of a cloister obviously had intentions toward another...her heart lay like a dead weight in her chest. She felt her feet thud on the floor as Burke led her onto the street. She felt his hand pawing her elbow.

"I need you to just listen to me, as a friend," Burke said.

Slowly she turned her face up to look into his. His eyes sparkled, and a tear spilling down and breaking up in his stubble shocked her back to the here and now.

"Goodness, Burke!" she gasped. "Whatever is wrong? Surely I..."

He shook his head. "No. I apologize for having led you on. I..." Fiercely, he brushed at his cheeks, and took a deep breath. "I...I was merely trying to make Ingrid jealous."

"Jealous?" Clara repeated dumbly. The bruising of her pride was tempered by a strange relief.

Burke put an arm around Clara, drawing her down into the darkening street. Clara was vaguely aware of the light dimming as a shadow blocked the glow from the tavern door for a moment. And the warm, muggy air shifted restlessly. Suddenly the music, the loud voices, all sounded so harsh and uncaring. Clara fell in step with Burke.

"I'll tell you as I walk you home," he said. But he stopped and gripped her shoulders, making her face him, their heads drawn close together, the way Ingrid and Jack had been speaking in the tavern. A sad little wave rippled over Clara, then sank back into the darkness. She turned her attention to Burke as he told her of his despair.

"Ingrid was—is still—a maid for a lady whom I served with my heart. Ingrid delivered our messages to and fro. But as is the case—the curse with us knights—I could not have her. At banquets, I used to gaze up to where her lady was sitting—I on the low table, and she up on the high table with my uncle—and...well, with time, I found myself falling in love with Ingrid. She, who used to pass messages between us." They began walking again, going slowly down the road toward the tailor shop and house. Clara listening with growing interest to Burke's story.

"Ingrid's messages grew fewer and fewer, as the lady in question was courted by a baron as well. And of course she chose him. But as he stole her from me, I found myself stealing Ingrid from her love, from her suitor. The journeyman, Jack Paisley."

"Ingrid and Jack were...courting?" Clara couldn't bring herself to suggest they were lovers. Her heart ached silently.

Burke shrugged. "As the lady chose the baron above me, so Ingrid chose me above a mere journeyman. Such are the shallow hearts of women, carelessly breaking those of men, all for the sake of security." He cast an accusing glance her way.

"How ironic! We women find you men equally heartless! Just as careless, and all in the name of...Dermot's favorite subject!"

Burke laughed, and Clara sighed, thinking how glad she would be to get out of this hurtful contest of love. Then she stopped and frowned.

"So, why did you and Ingrid not marry?" Clara asked.

Again Burke shrugged. "At first we waited for time to pass, for decency's sake. Then I realized that Ingrid, beautiful, lovely Ingrid, could capture any man's heart; she so charming."

"Yes, I know."

"I wondered if she would leave me for another, higher-ranking man? I worried that even I could not give her enough. I had spent so much time longing for that high table, I thought, if I could just...climb the ladder first, I would have more to offer her. Then, before I knew it, we had been lovers for years. In a way I had all I wanted from her already. Why marry?"

"Men!"

"However, just as I was about to propose to her, in came that Jack, returning to Godwick! Being so charming and so very decent, stealing her back from me!"

"How dare he!"

"Indeed!" Burke agreed, nodding earnestly. "And he is merely a tailor. Do you know what a fool I'll look when my men find out!" By now they had reached the tailor's door. "What am I going to do with her? How can I stop her from leaving me?"

"Has she not left you already?"

Burke blinked at her. "No. Not really, not until they are married, as such."

Clara sighed several times over as she wondered about Ingrid's intentions, remembering her bitter words, her strange behavior at the archery practice. She prayed that it wasn't wishful thinking on her part, but perhaps...mayhap... "I can only say, as a woman," she said at last, "that I suspect, by some of her gestures, some of the things she has implied, Ingrid *may* still have feelings for you... If my assumptions are correct, and she does still love you, she is angry with you. She is hurt because, in all this time, you've not... committed yourself to her..."

"But she knows I love her, surely!" Burke cried out, his voice echoing down the street earnestly. "I've shared her bed for..."

Clara held up her hand. "Please, spare me the finer details! Heed this, Burke; 'tis a silly thing with women, but out of the words *marriage bed,* we love the word *marriage* with the same degree of passion that men love the word *bed.* Women want to be proposed to officially, properly, romantically. And it is more than a question of security." She paused, and Burke nodded, frowning with concentration. "So what I'm saying is, if you ask her—clearly, and romantically—to *marry* you, and if she does still love you, then she'll forsake Jack, whom she may well be drawn to on the rebound. Indeed I hope so—I think so—and Ingrid will come back to you. So, declare yourself to her, and you could win her back."

"Do you honestly think so?"

Now it was Clara who shrugged. "There is a chance if you ask her. But there is no chance if you never do."

Burke stared at her for a moment. Then he grasped her shoulders and kissed her full on the lips. "Thank you, Clara! I shall ask her properly, with flowers. The day after tomorrow. On Saint Toole's parade day! You're a good friend!" He patted her back as he sprang back out into the street, almost knocking down an approaching figure. Another reveler returning home in the twilight, obscured from view in the shadows of the closely packed houses, and the gloom of the growing dark.

Clara paused in the doorway, feeling as blue as the inky, evening sky. I've made one person happy now, she thought, but I am in agony. And I'm bound to hurt at least another in the process. Either Ingrid will reject Burke, and that will hurt him deeply. On the other hand, if she accepts him, poor Jack will be spurned yet again! I would have a hand in hurting my dear Jack! Oh, how I hope she chooses him! And yet...No! God willing, please—no!

She wiped her hands across her cheeks. *Oh, Jack! Why can't you love me?*

"And you think you know someone..."

"Jack!" Clara squeaked, as the shadowy figure of the much aforementioned Jack sprang out of the gathering dark.

"I saw you!" He almost fell, catching himself with one hand on the door. He kept it there, leaning on it, his arm almost brushing her cheek.

"What?" Clara spluttered.

"You kissed him!"

"I did no such thing!"

"You *kissed* him! You are practically engaged to none other than *Christ*, and you cheat on him. In two days you're off to be a novice, a training nun, Clara, a *nun!* And I catch you canoodling in the street with...with army types!"

"I... No! *He* kissed *me*! And 'twas in gratitude, not..."

"I thought better of you than to have a need to sample such pleasures before settling down, but—sooth!—if you have *need* to, at least choose a *good* man. Never that woman-stealing, horny toad! That...that...Burke!"

Clara stared wide eyed at Jack. After a moment she said, "In truth, he's not so wicked when you know him properly. Although he is a bit daft, but..."

"Aha! So you've been sucked into his seductive charm, have you?" Jack cried. "Necking like a pair of swans in the inn...!"

"Necking! You exaggerate, sir! And he is truly pained at the way you and Ingrid have—"

"Before all guests in the public house, Miss *Novice Nun!*" Jack interrupted.

"We merely spoke; in the inn and out! Is it a sin to speak?"

"Ah, your tongue has let you down once again, Miss Clara, entwining, undoubtedly, with Burkes'."

With a stifled cry, Clara brushed his arm out of her way, causing him to lunge forward. He stopped his fall by catching hold of her arm and leaned in closer to Clara in a most unfamiliar way, his sour breath in her face.

"Why, you're drunk, Jack! You dare stand there, *drunk*, and lecture me on morality. Especially after I've seen you time and again like this..." She crossed her index and middle finger, shaking them in his face. "Like *this* with Ingrid. Keep your distance, Jack! You can have that dead Dermot's bed! And I hope you have nightmares and a splitting head in the morning."

Clara pushed the door open with her full weight. Still clutching her arm, Jack tagged after her into the shop, grabbing the lantern William had so thoughtfully left burning on the workbench and kicking the door closed. The light of the lamp lit his face from underneath, giving a chiseled and sinister quality to his appearance.

Breathing roughly and swaying slightly he said, "Hold your

tongue, you harpless hearty! 'Tis no fault of mine if Howard served me his strongest cider."

Clara laughed. "Harpless hearty?" She pushed him playfully in the chest, and he staggered backwards, catching onto the workbench. For a moment the only sound after their scuffle was the creek of the swaying lantern as the shadows stretched and shrank with its swinging. The flame spat and sputtered, but revived.

"I meant heartless harpy," Jack muttered.

A timid form darted out, and William emerged from the dancing shadows, white faced and round eyed.

"Please, sir, miss!" he squeaked, "Do not go upstairs. It's haunted there. Dermot's ghost is a-scratching, sir!"

Jack and Clara stared at William, and he stared imploring back at them. Jack steadied the lantern. He and Clara exchanged glances before he turned back to William and opened his mouth as if to speak, but a faint crunching bit into the silence. It sounded like distant footsteps on gravel.

"There! There he is!" William breathed.

Chapter Twelve

"Did you see him?" Clara asked. She held out her hand to William, and he came and stood in the crook of her arm.

"No, Miss Clara, I only heard him. He woke me up. I think he's under your bed."

Clara hugged William tighter.

"The vile man! Even in death—"

"Hush, Jack! Your words may bring him down here, clawing at our throats."

William squealed and buried his face in Clara's chest.

"—let me at him, I tell you! I have a mind for a brawl!"

"Jack! Hush!" Clara clutched at Jack's sleeve with her free hand. He all but shrugged her off and turned to William.

"What did he say, lad—shameful things?"

"I escaped downstairs and hid until you come back home."

"Oh, poor babe! We should not have left you all alone."

"What *says* he? Tell me each word!"

"He did not talk, sir: he's been a-scritching and a-scratching."

"Under my bed?"

"Or near it, miss."

Jack relaxed, and said with an unsteady wobble, which was easily mistaken for a swagger, "Ah, never fear, little Will! That's mice you heard."

Clara and William exchanged glances before turning their gaze on Jack.

William scratched his ear. "But master, it sounded...wrong, for mice."

"Rats, then!"

William shook his head.

"Do not argue with me! It's vermin, I tell you! Follow me—I shall show you!"

"Jack, no!"

Ignoring Clara, Jack took the stairs two at a time, the lantern swinging from his hand. Clara and William followed in his wake, their eyes fixed on the light, trying to ignore their grotesque shadows dancing along the walls. As Jack turned the corner of the first landing to go up the second, the light vanished for a moment, and darkness enveloped them. They whimpered as they hurried their steps, groping for the rope, and entered the loft room just as Jack put the lantern down on the floor with a thud. He drew his knife.

"Jack! That's for eating with!" Clara scolded in hushed tones.

But again he ignored her, or didn't hear. He dived onto his stomach, giving a sweep under the bed with his armed hand.

"Get on out, you pesky..."

An eerie yowl emanated from the depth. Clara and William jumped back, grappling franticly for one another. Jack cried out, and his shoulder knocked onto the underside of the bed as he propelled himself—or was propelled by some force, it was hard to tell. The yowl settled into a low threat of a growl as Jack, scrabbling backwards, drew his hand out. Attached to it was an enormous cat, biting at his arm, claws digging in.

"Why, it's a cat. It's just a cat!" Clara cried, her voice muffled as she put her hands to her mouth.

Sitting up, Jack beat the cat round its head with his free hand; it snarled and spat and boxed back at him. With its vicious teeth bared, its eyes yellow and glowing with malevolence, its tatty ears pulled back and its mouth and whiskers stained with the blood of a fresh kill, it looked beastly.

"Why, you little..." Jack made to throttle the cat, but it dodged out of his way with liquid motion, its front paws pummeling at him as it edged backwards.

"Jack, no!"

He made to hit at the cat again, but missed, and it shot back and curled itself up with a final snarl before leaping for the window. Within seconds it had squirmed through the shutters left ajar and disappeared into the night.

Clara rushed after it and watched as, having landed safely and with apparent ease on the roof of the house opposite, it trotted along the eaves before leaping across the next road, onto a roof beyond that. Clara turned back with a sigh.

"Oh, Jack, you frightened the poor thing away. We need a mouser."

Jack spluttered, looked at his scratched hand, his torn sleeves and back at Clara. "It attacked me!" he managed at last.

"Well, you disturbed it as it was eating. Never try to remove the food from an animal, or it will retaliate."

"Retaliate? It sprang upon me, savagely attacked me in the dark!"

"You attacked it first!"

"Woman...!"

"If you had left the cat at its business, there would be nothing for you to clean up. But no! You had to attack the poor thing with a knife. Now there is the corpse of a small creature under my bed, and who will fish it out? As you retrieve your weapon, I bid you take the little body with you."

Jack stamped his foot, almost overbalancing himself, and waved his bleeding arm at Clara. "You nagging *shrew*! I am bleeding, for the sake of rescuing you from ghouls, but you scold me for my efforts! You call that rabid beast a mouser—a *pet! And* I spied you consorting with Burke de Montforte. I've seen a side of you, Clara Baxter, that I never knew of. Now I understand how your father..."

Clara opened her mouth to retaliate, but William sprang between them.

"I will do it, sir! I will do it for you!" he said, scrabbling under the bed and bringing out a bloodied little mess.

"Indeed you shall, William; you are the apprentice!" Jack squared his shoulders and eyed the boy. "Besides, you seem to have a morbid taste for blood!"

"Yes, sir! It is more than half gone—its head is off. Why, that must have been the crunching sounds..."

Clara opened the shutters wide. "That's enough, dearest; throw it away, now!"

Jack groaned and put his good hand to his mouth. He took a few deep breaths. Clara cocked her head and bit her bottom lip. "Jack, I..."

But he glared at her and kept her at bay with his hand. "Good night!" he said coldly as he picked up a candle and lit it with the lamp.

Clara frowned as she watched him storm out, heard the trail of bumps as his feet slipped on the stairs, and his curse as he saved himself.

"This place does need a mouser," she muttered, pulling her bed curtains back.

"Pardon, miss?"

"Nothing, William. Let's to bed. It is very late, and my head spins."

"That will be my father's brew, Miss Clara."

* * * *

Jack knew the light of day was burning his eyes before he even opened them. His head throbbed, and his tongue felt puffy and dry as he tried to lick his cracked lips. He wanted to heave, he needed a pee, and he was parched enough to drain the city well. He would have rolled over and embraced the blank darkness of sleep once again, but the thought that he was lying in Dermot's bed sliced through his head like a sharp-bladed knife. He sat up and gagged, and groaned. Clara's feet thudded on the wooden floor as she crossed to the table set in front of the windows, heading for the hearth. She had opened the shutters, flooding the room with brightness, and waking him.

Through squinting eyes, Jack watched her as she scraped the old ashes from the fireplace, making iron screech against stone. She shifted the iron dogs noisily, and one of them hit the hearth with a crack that made him wince. He held himself up on one elbow and gazed blearily at her as she worked about, noisily getting the fire going again and setting some water to boil. Vaguely remembering the antics of the night before, he tried to gauge her mood, but his head ached and his eyes burned too fiercely for him to do any sort of thinking. She must have felt him staring at her, though, as she turned and smiled at him.

Well, he thought she was smiling genuinely, but then again...

He tried to speak. "Morning." It came out like a strangled caw.

"Good morning to you, sleepyhead!" she said brightly.

He frowned. She was definitely smiling, and he thought he heard her giggle. But was she being sarcastic or friendly? Was he experiencing the angelic forgiveness of the fairer sex, or the furious wrath of a woman scorned? She was back at her work, ignoring him. Or was she merely busy?

Jack tried to speak again, but it came out as a croak. He flopped back, causing his head to ache mercilessly, and sleep consumed him. When he woke again, realizing he'd been dozing, he opened his eyes wide. Sleep suddenly vanished as he thought of the daylight wasting away. Perhaps he'd only been asleep a few minutes.

Clara was still there, banging, thumping and clanging about with heavy iron and stone objects. Clonking wood against wood. He winced as she rushed suddenly across the floor toward his bed. She thumped a mug down at his bedside. He tried to read her face, but his eyes ached too much to stare. And her hair, frizzy from yesterday's plaits, hung about her face like a dark, glistening veil.

"Drink this," she said. "You'll feel better for it."

He couldn't distinguish her tone; it was soft and calm, as usual, but was it a little cool, a little flatter than normal? He could not be sure. His head felt too straw-stuffed to decide anything. He took the cup meekly and put it to his lips. It was some sort of herbal infusion, and it made him gag quite severely. He made to put the mug down.

"Uh, uh, uh!" she chided, "Drink it all up. No nonsense now! It's my grandmother's trusty remedy. It'll have you feeling better in no time." She pursed her lips and nodded meaningfully.

A cold wave of fear broke over him as the thought of poison crossed his mind. Or was that just a rather nasty wave of nausea?

The bed heaved as she sat down next to him, making his headache pulse violently in his skull, and he groaned involuntarily.

"Here, sip it slowly," she whispered. That was a gentle tone, to be sure, but right then, to him, it sounded as though she were hissing. "You were very drunk, you know," she said quietly, after a pause. "You were very nasty."

"Sorry," he croaked, foggy memories billowing back into his soggy brain. "God, yes, I'm sorry, my sweet..."

She put a cool finger on his lips. "Hush, now! Sip this up."

She held the cup to his mouth and helped him get some of the liquid down, though he gagged and spluttered. He felt truly wretched, inside and out.

"How are your hands? I apologize for being unkind to you about the cat. We had both of us drunk more than our fill," Clara said, pulling his rumpled jerkin over his head. He had not even undressed, he'd been so drunk. She laid his clean clothes on the foot of his bed for him, then set a basin of water for him to wash in.

"Harken," she said, "I have drunk of my grandma's brew, and I'm much improved already! I'll fetch you some more, and you rest a while longer. You'll begin to feel better soon."

"But, I was..."

She had left the room already. Jack could feel his aching head jar with each step she took. He got up slowly and washed his hand in scalding water. He was pleased to see that the welts were not overly red and did not burn with the heat of infection. The scratches were not as deep as he had expected, considering the size and ferocity of the cat. He bathed his hand a second time and rubbed some salve on it, just to make sure the wounds did not go bad.

By the time he made it down into the shop, the street outside was alive with bustling and hustling. Little William sat cross-legged on the workbench, working on the hand. He looked up as

Jack entered and smiled nervously.

"Miss Clara told me to finish the hand off while I waited for you to give me today's tasks," he said.

Jack came over and sat down stiffly before replying. "Good lad. I would like it to be finished today. How's it looking?"

William held it up for inspection. Jack squinted at it and turned it round and round again. Thanks to William's hard and imaginative work, the hand looked, in its gory detail, quite realistic, although it was four times the size of a man's hand.

"Is this not finished, then?" he asked.

"Almost, sir. Do you like it?"

"It's frighteningly accurate! Finish it off and take it to Father John after lunch. Clara can go with you."

* * * *

Unaware that she would be sent out in the afternoon, Clara quickly swept and tidied the solar and bedroom before coming quietly downstairs when she heard Jack talking with a customer. She slipped her pattens on and hurried out to the market, thus avoiding him. Her head was as muddled and busy with disjointed worries and nagging thoughts as the town square was with passersby. She stood absently, staring at a toad-swallowing performer nearby, while her mind swirled with last night's events. And she couldn't help feeling that accepting her lot in life was very much like swallowing a whole, live toad.

She was amazed to find that she could not feel any anger or resentment towards Jack. She had excused him and forgiven him. There was only a dull aching in her heart, which she assumed she would learn to block out entirely with prayer and grace. She knew she could not tell him of Burke's intentions toward Ingrid. Unless he told her, without any prompting, that he had no intentions toward the wretched girl herself. And she was sure he had.

She found she could not summon up any warm feelings for Ingrid this day. And that made her feel mean. What should it matter to her if the entire city of Godwick fell at Ingrid's feet? Her own life was set out so that no man would be a part of it, so should Jack stay single and alone because she couldn't bear to think of him with another woman? There had to be a sin in there somewhere. Oh, how she hated having to be so good! She almost resolved to be a very wicked nun indeed. And she watched, with all the gory fascination of a mind like little William's, as the toad swallower gagged and accidentally bit the leg off the toad as it went down his throat. His master beat him on the back angrily for making them look foolish. The poor pale lad heaved—very much like Jack had done earlier—as blood trickled from his mouth and spilt on the earth, next to the twitching limb.

Clara blinked and shook her head. What awful lives everyone seemed to have that day! She quietly slipped the swallower a grout as she walked away, endeavoring to concentrate on the errands she had to run.

When she returned to the shop, Jack was discussing weaves with a potential customer, so, taking off her pattens, she climbed noiselessly upstairs to set the table for lunch. Instead of a jug of ale, she had brought water. The thought of any brew—save her Grandmother's infusion—was distasteful to her that day. She also had a little bunch of wildflowers that she'd brought, more out of pity than for any other reason, from a ragged little girl in the market. She placed them in a little beaker next to the bread, breathing in their faint perfume as she set out the cheese and a bowl of nice Cox apples from the market. She sniffed them too as she shined them up, savoring their sharp fruity smell, pungent yet comforting in its homeliness. The sun broke through the clouds and stretched its bright fingers through the little window, illuminating the warm wooden boards, bouncing off the apples and making the cheese glow like amber.

Clara bit her lip. How sad she would be to leave this little solar, this house. She felt as though she'd been here for years. Already she knew each nook and cranny, which floorboards creaked, how many steps it took to reach the door, the window, the fireplace. This home had a warm and tender feel to it that needed no extra sunlight to brighten it, and this endeared it to her heart. She wished she could stay here forever, grow old sitting on the little stool by the fire, and climbing the stairs to the bedchamber above each night. This house seemed to cry out for a couple, a family, to live here as much as she yearned to fill it with baking and cleaning, and little children in smocks darned by her own hands.

She felt a hand brush past her hair. For a brief moment she thought it was Dermot, although she remembered he was gone even as she spun round to face him.

"Jack!" she gasped. "I didn't notice you come in!" He and William were staring intently at...not quite her...but something just above her head, in Jack's hand.

"You had a little spider in your hair," he said, quietly. He showed her the tiny creature, dangling from its invisible thread. Its spindly legs twitched, seeking a surface to grasp.

"It's a money spider," she breathed, staring in fascination at its swollen belly.

"Won't do to kill it," Jack said, hanging it over the flowers she'd set on the table. They watched as it flayed about until with grateful urgency, it found its footing and scuttled onto the delicate foliage.

"That's good luck to you." Clara smiled as they seated themselves at their places—*their places*—and Jack said grace.

They ate in silence for some time before he cleared his throat. "So...this will be your last full day here."

"Yes," Clara said, and after a stilted pause, she added, "it saddens me to go. I shall miss...Godwick, all the people, and..." Her voice trailed off. "Truly, I will!"

"I shall miss you terribly, Miss Clara," William said.

Jack stifled a cough. "Yes, we all will. Have you said your goodbyes to your new friends, or are you still going to do that?"

"Er..."

"I realize now, you were saying goodbye to Burke, which was why..."

"Oh, no! I...er...well, I gave him some advice. He asked me, so I gave it to him. Advice, nothing more. And he was so grateful that he...er..."

"Kissed you," Jack finished flatly. "Fine, good, I understand that...so, was he very grateful?"

"Yes, very." Clara paused to swallow down a sip of water, and another. "Woman's troubles. I mean the trouble men have with women. He didn't say who," she lied, "but I could guide him a little. And he was very grateful."

There was a long silence.

"Have another apple, dear William!" Clara picked the platter of apples and thrust it towards the boy so frantically that the top two apples wobbled and rolled off and onto the table. She snatched awkwardly at them several times, but only managed to send them spinning around on the surface as she continued to speak. "Burke was very emotional. We all were. Just a little over..." She gasped as Jack's hand, reaching for the same wandering apple as she was groping for, landed on hers instead.

"Yes," he said, "I regret the things I said." He looked directly into her eyes. "I apologize... William, fetch the hand and show it to Clara! He's done very well. It is finished now."

William dropped his knife onto the floor, he was in such a rush to obey, and as his feet echoed down the stairs, both Clara and Jack leaned over to pick it up.

"Let's forget all that was said," Clara whispered, "we were all a bit..."

"Burke," Jack interrupted, "...he didn't try...it *was* truly all about...what you said. I mean, he didn't ask you to..."

"Marry him? No! That was never a serious hint. No! And if he had...I would not have agreed. I want to be...to go to the convent, as my father said."

"Of course!" Jack turned away momentarily. "If you are sure! I mean, if you wanted to...if you did not wish to...I would never stop you."

Clara bit her lip. "But I think that is where my life is leading me."

"What I mean to say is...I wondered...I have been wondering if..." Jack began. But William burst in, making him start.

"Look! Miss Clara!" William carried the hand, now impaled, above his head. He had to hold the pole with both of his hands. Its outrageous proportions imbalanced him, making him stagger slightly. He peered round it too. Jack jumped up and helped him lay it on Dermot's bed.

Laughing, Clara admired it, "Excellent, work! How gruesome!"

"I wondered if you would like to take it with William to Father John?" Jack asked.

"Why yes, of course. How kind of you to think of me. I'd be honored to present it to him."

"We thought because you won't be able to walk with Jack when he carries it in the procession," William said, "you'd like to be the one to show it to him."

Clara grinned. "Ah, but *you* must do that, dearest," she said. "After all, you've done so much of the work on it, and it is very... detailed. Well done, William. I'm sure Father John will let you walk with Jack in the procession."

"Do you think so? Oh, do you really?"

"I shall have a quiet word with him myself," Clara said.

Chapter Thirteen

When Father John unwrapped the hand from the linen cloth, he put his hands to his cheeks.

"Surely, this is as it was," he breathed, running his fingers down the back of the hand and between the hanging ribbon tendrils. Despite grimacing and wiping his own hand across his chest, he continued in awed tones, "A hand so perfect and so sure. Built by God for the purpose of writing the word of God. A hand that not even death could destroy! Yes, this is a splendid job. I never thought I would see a hand to equal the one we lost, but this linen has worked well. Hark at the perfect, pale complexion of it."

William grinned and twiddling the dangling, morbid details. "See how real the red and purple and cream ribbons look, Father?"

Father John brushed his hand away lightly but agreed with a smile, "It resembles a severed hand, indeed! Ha, ha! Perfect! What a blessing! This will surely outshine any displays from the nuns of Saint Alba's Jawbone!" And he called his two curates to come and see.

"William's small hands were perfect for the finer details," Clara said. "He has worked most diligently at it."

"Then he must have some reward," Father John muttered.

Clara winked at William and smiled as she watched the men marvel at the fabrics and at the fine stitching. Father John chuckled with delight, and so did the boy and the young men. Gleefully they took turns holding the ghoulish display, admiring the colorful ribbons with their fine, realistic detail.

Father John let William hold the hand while he blessed it and sprinkled it with some holy water. Then he propped it upright in a corner by the reliquary that held Saint Toole's real hand.

William hurried back to the shop, but Clara lingered, asking Father if he had time to let her make another confession.

"But you confessed already this week, and you'll confess when you join the convent!" he cried.

"I know, but..." Clara trailed off and stared at him appealingly.

"Is it a mortal sin?"

"No...! I think not."

Father John shrugged. "Oh, very well, although I cannot imagine you would ever...you haven't committed a sexual act with a certain young man, or—Heaven forbid—did Dermot molest you on his deathbed?"

"No!" Clara winced at the thought. "But I feel it's my fault Dermot died," she said. "I washed him, I dunked him in that barrel, and then I put him outside."

Father John laughed and brushed her concerns aside as though he were swatting at gnats. "Nonsense! You did your best for him."

She confessed that she'd fallen asleep while keeping watch over him on the night he passed away. "I'm a poor excuse for a nurse. What sort of nun will I make?" she said, wringing her hands as Father John studied his fingernails, intermittently scraping their undersides clean with his incisors.

"Stop beating your breast over nothing!" he said.

"But I feel so wretched," she whined. "And actually, a man kissed me last night."

At that, Father John looked up. "You kissed a man!"

"It wasn't a romantic kiss," Clara said, "it was a gesture of thanks. Like the sign of peace we offer one another at Mass."

"Humph! I've a thing or two to say about that!"

Clara sighed. "But the thing that troubles me, Father," she said after a moment of contemplation, "is that another man, appointed by my father as my guardian, he saw and was angry because he thought it was...a romantic gesture. But how do I know if this man is angry because he cares for me in a...special way? Or if he is angry because he loves me as a brother and wishes to see me remain pure and chaste before going into the convent? And the man who kissed me to thank me loves a woman whom I suspect my guardian loves. And she may still love him. But I told the man who kissed me to ask her to marry him, because he told me he still loves her as well. And I thought she may love him rather than my guardian. However, I cannot know how she feels. And if he does ask her and she does love him, then my guardian, whom I ...adore...and wish the best, may lose her. And it will be my fault. I have to ask myself; did I advise him to do that because I don't want him to be with her? Because...I want him to be with me."

"Who?" Father John frowned and ran his hands over his bald patch. "The man who kissed you?"

"No! The other. But I shouldn't be loving *anyone*, should I? I should be..." Her words trailed off.

Father John rubbed his face and sighed. "No, you should not

be falling in love." Then he asked, "Clara, had anyone been at the ale?"

She confessed that they all had. Quite a bit.

"Now you see, the Devil's work was at hand! Too much drinking and too much kissing has led to all this confusion in your mind." He leaned forward and lowered his voice as he continued, "You should see the parishioners lining up for confessions after holy days! I keep telling them, holy days are for worship and reflection, not drunkenness and debauchery. Go into that confessional and I'll take your confession properly!" he ordered.

She obeyed, and once she had repeated her muddled ramblings, Father John said, "Your guardian was angry only because he means to deliver you into the hands of the convent in a pure state. Cast these romantic notions out of your heart! Steep your mind in prayer, and try to be grateful that you will soon be protected from all the confusion that courting brings. You have reminded me of why I became a priest myself! It's obviously God's will that you join the convent. Now make an act of contrition..."

He absolved her abruptly and gave her a penance that kept her praying in the knave for half an hour.

Although Clara left the church believing that she was fully resolved to go happily into the Convent of Saint Alba's Jawbone, a sudden recall stirred everything up into a tangle again.

She was passing the spot where the toad swallower had made his bloody folly, and she found herself looking on the ground to see the severed leg. It was no longer there, of course. Some dog or crow had undoubtedly scavenged it, or—she thought with a chuckle—some macabre little boy may well have picked it up and put it in his pocket. All that remained of the incident was the browning bloodstains, little dark spots on the beaten earth, which she wouldn't have noticed if she hadn't been looking.

As she resumed her walking, a picture of the retching toad swallower flashed across her mind's eye, which led her to think of Jack's liverishness that morning. She smiled fondly as she remembered... Then she stopped dead in her tracks, motionless for a moment, so that a large-breasted woman bumped into her from behind.

"Take care!" the woman retorted, pushing past her irritably.

But all Clara replied was, "He said, 'my sweet.' He called me 'my sweet'! Did he not?" The corners of her mouth lifted slightly; then a grin slowly spread across her face. It seemed Jack loved her after all, rather than Ingrid. And as for Ingrid, Burke would soon be asking her to come back and marry him. Why wouldn't she? A sheriff was a better bargain than a poor tailor. Oh, how beautiful the streets of Godwick looked that afternoon! How warmly she smiled at the water carriers. A couple of passing soldiers were heroic guardians of the town, and how romantic they looked as they winked at the pretty maidens in the street.

The solid town walls wrapped around the mushroom huddle of homes and shops in a loving embrace, and each building with its quaint rickety frame leaned comfortably on its neighbor for support. In the market the linen displays of the cloth merchant were bright and gay, as were the pyramids of the seasonal vegetables, Mother Huckle's soaps and remedies, even the beggars' rags. All over the town, splashes of color rang out in the market and spilled from the shops onto the cozily narrow streets.

The children's voices and those of their scolding mothers were like choirs of angels. People smiled lovingly at one another, blessing each other as they passed in the glorious avenues, dotted not with rotting cabbage leaves but with fragrant rose petals.

Clara hummed her favorite hymn in a perfect soprano all the way back to Jack's darling little shop, and was just easing her butterfly-light feet out of her pattens, when she came crashing back down to earth.

Behind the door, Ingrid's pattens were cuddling up to Jack's, and her laughter came tinkling from way back in the darkest, furthermost corners of the shop. Possibly from the storeroom right at the back. Or—worse—perhaps they were drifting down from the solar. That same room she had that very morning dreamed would be a home, with she and Jack as the family within. That boudoir of Dermot's where he'd lain and emanated his lustful thoughts. Clara picked her pattens up, ready to put them on and retreat back into town. But she thought if she could catch a snippet of their conversation, mayhap she would be proved wrong. She found herself creeping up on the pair, her eyes and ears straining, her heart pounding expectantly in her chest.

She saw them in the back of the shop. William was way back in the storage area, sorting or packing fabric into a trunk. Farther forward, Ingrid was standing in the opening of the little curtained-off changing area, and Jack was touching her shoulders. They were so engrossed in each other, they didn't notice as Clara watched him running his hands down Ingrid's arms. He was saying something, murmuring in his quiet way; she couldn't catch his words. Even Ingrid, her eyes lit up in what could only be love and her lips parted in a seductive smile, had to lean her face closer to his in order to hear. Clara stifled a gasp as something about Jack's ways struck her. She always thought he was shy and gentle, more sensitive than most men, but was this soft-spoken manner of his a ruse to make his audience all the more attentive? Oh, what a cunning, seductive hunter he was!

She stepped back, crept backwards silently until she reached the staircase, then tiptoed up it. How could she have been so wrong in her judgment of him; how could she have been so misled? She moved toward the bed, intent of flinging herself down and having a good cry. But it was Dermot's bed. And her tears wouldn't come. She stepped across the floorboards as lightly as she could, so as not to make them creak. She needed some time for quiet contemplation, for absolute solitude.

Below her, even the faintest of movements could be heard.

* * * *

Jack had been murmuring about the fit of her new sleeves when Clara had spied them. Ingrid had gushed her gratitude and promised him, "I'll show them off to everyone I know, and anyone who happens to notice them. 'These,' I shall say, 'are the fine work of the tailor, Jack Paisley!'"

Jack blushed and allowed this important first customer to slip her hand under his elbow as he led her back to the front of the shop, with William in tow.

"Master Jack!" William whispered urgently in the moment's quiet, "Listen!"

They all paused in their step and were duly rewarded with the creaking of a floorboard. They eyed each other in silence, and a rustle, followed by another creak filtered down from upstairs.

"Clara must be back," Jack suggested. But he was whispering.

All eyes looked toward the entrance, where pattens were habitually removed.

"Her pattens aren't there," William breathed.

Ingrid glanced about her, clutched at Jack's arm. "What if it is the ghost of Dermot?" she hissed.

"Nay, never! It must be Clara," Jack said aloud, breaking away from Ingrid's grasp. "I shall go and investigate."

"No! I beg you would not leave me!" Ingrid howled dramatically, grabbing at Jack's arms, pulling him back. "You go, William," she ordered. "You're not afraid, are you?"

Jack frowned, but William rose to the challenge instantly.

"No fear! Why last night we thought it was the same, but it was only a cat!" he said, but his chin was a little too high, his shoulders a trifle too squared to ring true as he ran up the stairs. He slowed down when he came toward the top and flinched as something creaked within the solar.

"Clara?" Jack called, his foot already on the first stair.

* * * *

It was, of course, Clara. She'd heard William's words clearly as he bounded upstairs, followed by Jack. In retrospect, she realized she should have called back, telling them it was indeed her. But guilty at having crept away from them, and desperately wanting to be alone to lick her wounded heart, she felt compelled to hide. And she pressed herself flat against the wall, beside the chest that stood in the doorway. She was, indeed, half hidden by the trestle table, pushed up against the wall and to her right, between the doorway and herself. With the open shuttered windows letting the light stream in blindingly, and with William being unnerved, he didn't spot her. Being a child still, and not very good at looking for things, he glanced in and gasped at the apparent emptiness, the confirmation of his fears.

From below came the sudden movement of Jack as he, obviously alarmed by William's frightened reaction, bounded up the last of the stairs. Ingrid, also set off by their reactions, screamed as Jack left her farther behind, increasing the tension a hundred fold all round. If William had remained rigid at the spot in the doorway, Jack would have undoubtedly seen Clara when he got to the doorway but he didn't get there.

William turned and bolted down, yelling, "It's Dermot's ghost, to be sure! I could hear his breathing! But I saw nothing!"

He crashed into Jack, who was on his way up, and it was all he could do to grab the boy by the shoulders as they both fell back. Their fall was broken by Ingrid, who ran up after Jack as she screamed. They all tumbled down and landed in a tangled heap in the shop. It was while they were picking one another up and Jack crying, "Calm yourselves! Don't panic!" that William squealed.

He said tearfully, "It's his ghost come back to haunt us!" And he immediately launched into a graphic account of how the bedding was heaving up and down as though breathing of its own accord, to the sound of Dermot's strangled gasping, with Ingrid whimpering as she hung on each one of his imaginative words.

* * * *

Clara heard the commotion quite clearly downstairs as she pressed herself against the wall. Again she had the chance to come out of hiding and at least pretend that she'd been accidentally positioned out of William's sight at the crucial moment of his entering the solar. But she was aware she had just given them quite a fright, and along with her morose heartache she felt a fresh, stronger flood of guilt and awkwardness. Instead of revealing herself, she continued to hide. Indeed, she felt it imperative that she do so; she could only imagine acute embarrassment upon being discovered.

While the three below were occupied with untangling themselves, Clara scrambled up to the third floor. To the room where she slept, to the comfort of her own things. She would have liked to throw herself on her bed and tell anyone entering the room to leave her alone; she had a sense that this was all very silly, but wasn't listening to the voice of reason at that moment. She was too busy fleeing. The idea had formed in her muddled head that she needed to sneak out unseen, and re-enter the building as though for the first time. Then her mortification would pop like a bubble on a bramble thorn and all would be well. Better still, she would have a secret smile at their expense. A wicked ripple of vindication scurried through her bones. It was the only pleasant feeling around, and she grabbed at it as desperately as Ingrid clutched at Jack downstairs.

Clara listened for a moment and heard Jack's voice, and Ingrid's and Jack again, and the sound of footsteps. They were coming up again, getting closer. They would re-investigate the solar; then, undoubtedly, they would come and inspect this room for the source of the ghostly noises. Her heart leapt as she heard the words, "...devil of a cat...," and, "...up in the attic room..." from Jack. And footsteps again, just below her.

The linen sheeting Jack had set up as a partition for her had been taken down, leaving the room open and exposed. Even as she hurried to the barrels, crib and other paraphernalia on the farthermost side of the room, she pictured Jack and William searching through all that for their "huge" rats and "devil of a cat." And if she were found blatantly hiding, that would be far too embarrassing. No, she could not be found there! She had to exit the house unseen and re-enter as though just then returning. Stroking the roof of her mouth with her scarred tongue, Clara looked across the room at the window.

"Aha! Did you hear that?" Jack's voice reached the upstairs room. "If that cat has ventured back, I'll..."

Stifling a gasp as she heard his footsteps fast approaching the ladder, and those of Ingrid and William shuffling behind his, Clara bolted for the window. She crouched on the sill, holding the frame and focusing on the roof opposite theirs, her eyes widening at the distance between the roofs. That very cat Jack was cursing had made it effortlessly, and Clara had always imagined she could reach out and touch the opposite tiles, but now it seemed so far. Too far. The thud and bustle of the approaching company set her heart pounding, and in a single wild beat she sprang with all the velocity of a flea abandoning a sheep bound for the dip.

Chapter Fourteen

"See?" Jack smiled, opening his arms to the still and empty room. "There are no spirits here!"

Ingrid and William huddled behind him in the doorway, jumping violently at the sound of a scream, and a man's voice crying out in alarm down in the street. They all glanced involuntarily at the window. It stared back impassively at them, letting in only cloud-filtered light from above and the echoes of feet and voices from below. Jack strode over to the window and, leaning on the sill, gazed down at the street. Noticing nothing untoward for a busy weekday, he turned his attention back to the question of their ghost and crossed to the bed. His face was placid as he bent down and looked under it.

"No sign of that cat," he said. He gave William, pale and wide eyed, a quick smile as he got up and crossed to the barrels and began shifting them about. "I warrant you, if we have a look here, we shall find a rat or two to answer for all this noise. And for the cat's attraction to this room."

Ingrid sighed and sat down on Clara's bed, watching as William hurried forward to help Jack.

It wasn't long before with a cry of triumph, Jack stopped and pointed. "Hark at that!" He shook his head.

"What is it?" "Let me see?" Ingrid and William cried together, struggling over the increasing clutter of shifted items.

For an instant, as their eyes lit upon Jack's discovery, they stared dumbly.

"Oh, dear," Ingrid said at last, "a cradle? Whose is it?"

"Look within it," Jack said, "in amongst the linen..."

Ingrid bent down, her hand reaching into the old clothes and sheets. She recoiled suddenly. "Ugh! A nest! A rat's nest!"

Jack gazed into the cradle. "That's what comes of keeping this sort of thing, rather than passing it on to another, more fortunate set of parents. Now it's good for nothing–look how this fine little vest has been chewed."

"How long has the nest been there?" William asked, creeping in for a closer look.

"Not too long. Clara mentioned the cradle, but never a word of it having tenants," Jack replied, stepping back to let William get a good view.

The boy bent down and stared into the cradle, shifting aside some nibbled fabric to properly expose a little brood. He poked at their writhing pink bodies. "Where are the parents—do you think the cat was eating their mother?" he asked. "Do we have to kill the babies now? How shall we do it, Master Jack? Shall we drown them?"

Jack rubbed his brow and stared out of the window. "I suppose. I don't know," he mumbled. "Clara's right; we have need of the services of a cat. A good mouser."

"Ugh!" Ingrid sniffed, peeking at the nest from a safe distance. "But, Jack, how could such tiny little things have made so much scratching and thumping?"

Jack merely cast her a blank look. She shrugged and turned to go, saying, "Well, of course you shall have to kill them now. As soon as you leave the room, the mother will come out of hiding and move them, and then..."

"I'll kill them for you," William volunteered. "Shall I throw them into the fire? Or the river?"

"No! Not the fire." Jack shuddered. He coughed and gave his chin a scratch. "Er...Clara may be upset if she sees them. She has a tender heart, that lass."

Ingrid wrinkled up her nose. "Well, I will leave you to your little domestic dilemma. See me out, Jack. Oh, and, Jack," she said, pausing to fix him with an alluring stare, "congratulations on your inheritance. This is fine indeed!" She indicated the room with a sweep of her hand, "How does it feel to have such an eligible bachelorhood thrust upon you?"

He stared thoughtfully at her for a second. "Me a...? Why, yes, I reckon that does change..." he mumbled, fell silent for moment, then broke his stillness as he indicated the door. "Er...this way."

Laughing, she tucked her hand in the crook of his arm.

* * * *

Wedged rather uncomfortably into Clara's elbow, meanwhile, was the rough hand of a soldier. And what gave this arrangement such a high level of discomfort was the fact that the soldier was pushing her arm up between her shoulder blades as he frogmarched her toward a heavy wooden door.

"I beg you," Clara squealed, her plaintive tones echoing off the thick, damp walls, "if only you would allow me an audience with the Sheriff Burke de Montforte!"

The soldier laughed and said something she couldn't take in. Her ears were too busy registering the coarse laughter of men rebounding down the corridor. She heard footsteps—hard, masculine steps marching above her scuffling footfall. She heard the chink and scrape of metal thrust into metal and the plink of water dripping on stone, smelled the ragged scent of masculine sweat and old leather mingling with the rasp of mildew. And she felt the chill of gray stone walls, damp and stark.

"I demand an audience with Burke de Montforte!"

Feet skidded. A moment of stillness and silence followed.

"Good Lord, Clara, what are you doing in custody?" a familiar voice asked.

It was then Clara realized that she had shut her eyes tightly. She opened them and found herself gazing into the face of none other than the aforementioned Burke de Montforte. He winked at her.

"Oh, thank you—why, thank you! Oh, praise be to God!" she said, to her escort, to Burke and to the good Lord.

"This woman was discovered trespassing, in the house of one Mr. Gimmer, the tailor. In the upstairs part of the house," the soldier said bluntly.

Burke's eyes widened considerably. "Clara, is this so?" he breathed.

"I can explain!"

"Mrs. Gimmer was witness to the young woman gaining entrance through the window of the upstairs house. She was pursued out of the house and into the streets before being arrested."

"Here is the truth of the matter," Clara said. "I was attempting to climb onto the roof. I meant no harm and certainly had no intention of crashing in through the window."

"You had a mind to jump onto the roof of Mr. Gimmer's house?" Burke asked.

"Yes! No...! Well..." Clara thought quickly. "I was in the throes of capturing a cat. A great, fierce cat on the roof. My cat...it was sitting there on the roof. The cat of the house I live in. It had been missing, and we need it, for 'tis an excellent mouser. But it was gone for...er...days, and then out of my window, I spied it...sitting on the roof So I...without a thought for my safety, I sprang out of the window, after the cat."

After a pause, she added, "I was very desperate."

"I am certain you were! But why did you not call it by name?"

Clara glanced heavenward briefly before replying, "It would not come to me. I *did*...I did call it. But it moved to go on and I... jumped after it." Then she added sincerely, "However, I missed, landing not on the roof, kind sir, but rather, I caught the guttering with my hands and hung there. I feared I would to fall to my death! But I saved myself by swinging my legs, and thus I went through the window. My intrusion was unintentional."

Clara swiped her scarred tongue over the roof of her mouth and looked at Burke. Burke looked at the soldier.

"'Tis as Mrs. Gimmer says," the soldier informed him, "that she came in through the window feet first."

"And the cat?" Burke asked.

The soldier afforded only a blank stare.

"Gone," Clara replied quickly.

Burke's hand rested on the hilt of his sword, absently swinging back and forth for a moment.

"Unhand this woman," he said. "I know her, and I believe her story's true. She is a reliable woman, all but gentry. Her father is a wealthy merchant in the town of Winchester. She is awaiting the pilgrim to Saint Alba's Jawbone, that she might join the march and become a novice at the convent."

The soldier dropped her as though she were hot coals.

As Burke escorted her out, Clara prayed that he wouldn't ask any revealing questions. However, walking beside her towards the doorway, he inquired, "Incidentally, Clara, what color is your cat?"

She licked her lips, trying to recall the cat that had fought with Jack. "He is gray and stripy. A tabby! 'Tis a wild thing, that cat. That is the reason it ran away."

Burke stopped in his tracks. Clara's heart seemed to stand still too.

"I remember my men talking about a tabby that's been stalking the ramparts recently," he said.

Clara's heart collapsed down into her queasy belly, and a tiny "oh" escaped her lips as she raised her eyebrows daintily at Burke.

"They have been trying to kill the brute for about a week now, but he's too nimble," he continued. "Nasty, vicious cat. He launches remarkable, sudden attacks. Leaps out onto them from the shadows and claws them like a demon, and then disappears into the night. But I have a cunning plan to trap the fiend. I was going to drown him, but I shall return him to you."

Clara nodded in thanks and fixed her eyes the door ahead of them. The corridor seemed to narrow and darken around the heavy wooden door, and daylight filtered in underneath and around the jar of it, like an illuminated halo. They walked in silence for a moment.

As they were passing through the doorway, Burke suddenly stopped and asked, "He is a tom, your cat, or is he a female?"

Clara grimaced, her heart tightening up again. "Ooh, I don't know...a male I suppose. Er...because it's never had kittens. Unless he ate them—she ate them! As you said, 'tis an enormous and vicious cat."

"Must be the one!" Burke concluded with a click of his fingers. He grinned and winked at her, promised to bring her cat back to her if they succeeded in catching it. Then he guided her out the doorway, into the muggy embrace of the free town. She mumbled her good-byes and, almost falling down the stairs, hurried into the streets.

She ran all the way home.

* * * *

Just a few hours later, Clara sat before the window like a spider in her web, darning a tear in her surcoat. The picture was serene if not beautiful. She sat in her kirtle on a stool positioned where the dying day threw the last of its soft light, fading from long golden-fingered rays into a blue haze. Gradually the blue would darken into the inky night sky.

Clara glanced out over the rooftops at the sky and quickened her stitching, leaning over the russet fabric, tilting it to get the best of the light. Her face was calm, and it seemed a smile played at the corners of her mouth. But she bit her bottom lip from time to time, and her hands trembled as she worked. Although her hair looked charmingly soft, tumbling out of her plaits in wispy curls, it was evidence of her chase, of her nonsensical little secret. A fib that seemed to lead, like stepping stones over a torrent of guilt, from one little deception to the next, to the next.

Jack, blissfully unaware of her earlier exercise in deception, paused in the doorway and looked at her fondly, thinking of how honest and gentle she was. How pious and obedient. No wonder it seemed that God had chosen for her to spend her life in prayer, glorifying His name. Jack wondered if she thought him good enough to swap such a life for one with him. His heart beat against his chest, and his hands, too, felt unsteady as he approached her.

"Clara, I beg you not to fill your last hours here with work," he implored her gently. "Why not rest a while?" He pulled up a stool and sat opposite her, drew the stool closer still, so that if they both bent forward their heads would touch. Their knees had no space worth mentioning between them.

Clara jumped, and her needle pierced her. "Oh! You frightened me!" She sucked her finger, the metallic smack of blood making her grimace.

"I'm sorry!" He grabbed for her hand, but her needle was sharp and somehow got in the way. They both were pierced. He leaned back, his hands on his knees. She leaned back, her eyes on her work.

"I want to mend this tear," she said, and her hands moved again, busily and quickly, as she darned.

"How did it happen?"

She shrugged. "I know not." Another lie. She was keeping count. Her next visit to the confessional would be a long and fruitful one.

"Let me do it for you," he offered, reaching for her hands again.

She hurried her last stitch. "But, see, I am done!" she said quickly, then after a moment, she added, "Thank you, nevertheless!" She tensed the thread and made to bite it off, but Jack pulled a scissors from seemingly nowhere.

"Tut, tut, tut!" he chided with a smile, and she resigned to let him snip the thread for her. For a moment she looked into his eyes, and the pain it caused in her heart was sharp and searing. She swallowed and turned away, gazing out the window.

Jack rubbed his hand across his chin. "William...er...where is the brown woolen cloth Mr. Emmert chose?"

William looked up, his mouth gaping for a moment, before he replied with a frown, "All laid out for cutting in the morning, sir."

"Well...go down and look upon it, please?"

William shifted a little farther away from the adults. "Look upon it, sir?"

"Yes...er...place these scissors beside it ready for the morning too."

"Very good, sir," William said. He took the scissors from Jack and made for the door. There he hesitated and turned. "But sir, I'm a little afraid. The ghost..."

"That was rats! Have no fear, boy!" Jack said quickly. Then he smiled encouragingly. "Go on! Take a candle then! Be gone!" and he shooed William with silent hands as he mouthed, "Go! Now!"

Frowning, William hurried downstairs, leaving the adults properly alone.

Jack cleared his throat. By William's hurried footsteps, he gauged he had only seconds to get to the point. But it was not the sort of point he was confident enough to lunge at. Like needles, it could pierce sharp and sore.

He cleared his throat again. "Clara, now that I've...that is, I think we be close enough for me to enquire...do you believe me now as...eligible?"

There was a horrid silence. Clara turned her face away from the light of the window; the room seemed to have grown as dark as a well.

Staring unseeing, with a wave of bitter resentment sweeping over her, she swallowed and managed to ask levelly, "Do you ask of me, if I...do you wish to know if perhaps...some...woman would like to marry you?" She couldn't bring herself to mention Ingrid's name.

"Er...well, yes, you could put it that way," Jack mumbled and ducked his head.

Clara narrowed her eyes, sure it was guilt rather than shyness she detected in his voice. "If you wish to...know. If the time is right," she said, "why do you not ask?"

Jack found himself swallowing hard. There was something cold and decidedly uninviting in Clara's tone. And her eyes seemed, eerily, to bore straight through him. He put it down to his own nerves.

"I am trying...I will...but I have a mind...she...may not want... marriage."

Clara guffawed. "Most women do."

"Aye, but what of...what is your opinion?"

"What of it, what does it matter?" she answered quickly.

"I know your father...but you seem..." Jack faulted under her gaze. He drew a lungful of air and began again. "Clara, do you really wish to go to the Convent of Saint Alba's Jawbone?"

Clara rose up, holding her mended surcoat in front of her, ready to slip it over her kirtle. She drew her breath and silently counted her next lie, "Oh, yes, indeed! It is my wish to be a nun in the convent of Saint Alba's Jawbone." And she managed a smile.

Jack stood up to reach out for her, but his hands didn't seem to know where to go, and after hesitating, he placed a hand on her shoulder. Now it was he who seemed to have trouble looking into her face. "As you wish," he whispered huskily.

"Master! Master Jack!" William yelled, thumping up the stairs. "There's a soldier—the sheriff—at the door!"

Clara gasped. She glanced round eyed at Jack, bit her bottom lip, put her hands over her face. When she peeked out from between her fingers, Jack was following William down to the shop. She threw her surcoat over her head, whipped her girdle around her waist, and, tying her purse in place, she hurried after them, thinking fast.

When she got to the bottom of the stairs, Burke was in the doorway, William and Jack looking tentatively on. Burke was disheveled. A thin line of drying blood traced its way down his right cheek, and the stuffing of his gambeson was bursting out of two long tears. His brow was shiny and his cheeks were flushed, while his eyes bore the sparkle of fresh victory. His hands were protected by newly scratched leather gloves, and clasped in his right hand, tied securely shut, was a writhing bag. He held it at arm's length.

"I have it, Clara," he grinned, as she entered, "I found your cat."

Jack frowned. "Cat?"

"Why, thank you so much!" Clara quickly pushed her way forward and took the bag from Burke. "Allow me pay you..."

Burke held up his free hand. "Not at all. We were glad to get rid of it!"

"Rid of it?" Jack murmured, looking around for answers. But Clara and Burke were intent on the bag, which went still as he handed it to her. Only William seemed keen to meet his master's eye, and he frowned and shrugged dramatically.

Clara positioned herself between them and the sheriff and boldly invited him in, but he eyed the bag and stepped backwards.

"No, I fear I cannot...I must attend a meeting about the parade...so..."

"Thank you! Thank you so much!" Clara said, edging towards him with the bag. He almost tripped backing out of the door. "Well, goodbye!" she called ever so politely after him. Clara quickly shut the door and turned to her companions with a smile.

"Well, lads," she said with deliberate charm, "I have here, in this bag a...departing gift for you! Just what you need." The bag growled a low, curdled warning. Jack and William stared at it and edged back. Clara swallowed and grinned apologetically at how easy this fib—a mere half truth—slid off of her tongue. "I have heard scufflings and scratches...and thumps and bumps, as

I'm sure you have. And I believe we have rats. So I...acquired...a mouser!"

She set the bag down on the floor and untied the knotted end.

Chapter Fifteen

The bag trembled, hesitated, twitched tentatively, then ceased once again to move. After a terse moment, William leaned forward, closer. It burst into life again. With a menacing growl the tatted tip of a feline ear bobbed up from the dark hole of the mouth. Two paws, claws extended, flayed viciously at the sacking, and a yowl reverberated through the darkening room. Slashing, snarling and biting its way into the room, the gray tabby tore from its prison, launching a frenzied attack on the bag, and the immediate stretch of flooring. Jack, Clara and William, stood watching it, hands clasped at their chests, mouths slightly parted. Then the cat stopped, its long razor claws etching the floor, its bristling back arched and its tail raised and flicking. Its narrowed green eyes glared dangerously at the surrounding company.

"Holy Mary, Mother of God!" William squeaked, genuflecting rapidly.

"*Shh*!" the cat hissed, batting at the boy's leg. Its eyes glinted in the light of the candle, reminding them all that nighttime was creeping in like a black tide.

William clapped a hand over his mouth and froze, his blue eyes glistening and round. The cat, still focusing on him, changed its position from crouching to standing with a ripple of muscles, glaring all the while.

"'Tis possessed," William whispered behind his hand. "Do you think it's possessed?"

After a moment's hesitation, Clara said very softly, "No! I think the poor creature is frightened."

The cat's chipped ears twitched, and with a barely visible turn of its head, it turned its eyes on Clara.

"Oh, aye!" Jack muttered sarcastically, "It's more scared of us than we are of it."

The cat turned its attention to Jack now, seemingly without moving. Its pink tongue slid out of its mouth, and it yawned, revealing a row of needle-long, needle-sharp teeth, its long tail flicking back and forth. The tip of the serpentine tail, Clara noticed, was permanently bent. As its fur began to subside, the cat showed its true leanness. Its shoulder blades stuck up like wing buds, its waist was pinched as though tightly laced, ribs visible.

"Hark at that! There is a gentle side to this pitiable creature," Clara said.

Jake studied the cat through narrowed eyes for a moment before replying. "Aye? I am looking for it."

Clara sighed. "I thought you could do with a mouser. Indeed, I've said so a number of times. And see how hungry this poor wretch is—it could do with a home."

Jack grunted an agreement and turned to go. The cat gave a sudden, loud yowl and launched another attack. All jumped, Jack whipping round to face the beast, but the cat's target was the sack. Hissing and growling, it mauled the bag by dancing on it with bared claws and arched back. Clara, Jack and William watched in fascinated horror at the brutal assault before, moving as one, they began to tentatively retreat, walking quietly towards the stairs.

"I'll put down the last of the milk for it," Clara breathed, "to encourage it to stay."

"I think it may prefer blood."

"It will?" William asked, his eyebrows arched.

The cat suddenly stopped its attack, and in the ensuing silence everyone froze. It stared at them with luminous eyes, and they stared back.

"Meow!" it said gruffly at last, showing again a row of sharp herringbone teeth. One eye seemed smaller than the other, as though in the act of a perverted wink. Haughtily, the cat turned its side to the crumpled, defeated sack and sprayed on it.

"'Tis a boy," William announced.

Jack pursed his lips and shook his head slightly. "Thank ye kindly," he said to Clara, "for this wonderful parting gift."

"You shall thank me in the morning, when it...*he*...has kept the mice away from your materials!" Clara quipped, as they turned to go upstairs.

The cat sprang, rudely pushing past Jack and Clara, and ran ahead of them up to the solar.

"If he sprays upstairs, I'll wring his neck," Jack muttered. He picked up the sack and threw it outside into the gutter before following Clara and William.

When Jack arrived in the solar, the cat was already finishing the last of the milk. Then as Clara tidied their littering of the day, the cat followed her about and kept rubbing his face against her legs. When she stepped away from him, he lunged himself at her calves and rubbed his face deep into her skirts, gripping at the material with both front paws—claws out, of course—thus outlining the shape of her legs. Once or twice she staggered heavily under his advances, and did at last fall down.

"You imp!" she cried before succumbing to laughter. As she sat upon the floor in a fit of giggles, her arms behind her, trapped in bearing her weight with her knees bent, the cat lunged at her with renewed vigor, practically batting his face into her chest, arms, neck and face. It was like being molested.

"Stop it!" Clara said, turning her face this way and that to get away from his advances, "You're worse than Dermot—God rest his soul!"

"Get off!" Jack said, trying to push the cat aside.

In a flash the cat whipped out his claws and scratched Jack's arm, nipping him, before turning back to Clara in one fluid motion and continuing his tenacious advances. Jack stared, his hands pulled in onto his chest, and his face very still.

William asked, "Do you think he's going to spray on you, Miss Clara?"

Clara hurled herself up in an instant, and with such obviously God-given strength that the animal spun around on the floor, his paws splaying out. He regained his footing, shook his head and lunged himself at Clara's legs again.

"I believe him to be younger than he looks," she panted, taking a candle and lighting it. She limped across the room, the cat clinging onto her.

Jack nodded as he crossed to the window to close the shutters. He kicked tentatively at the cat as he passed—a mere gesture. The creature responded by hurling himself from Clara's skirts to Jack's leg, where he stuck like a burr, chewing thoughtfully on one of the leather straps of his hose.

"What shall we call him?" William asked, and, crouching down, he urged the cat to come to him with little hand gestures and soft clicking.

"Beelzebub," his master suggested, trying to shake the cat off. The cat growled and dug his claws in deeper, causing Jack to wince. But almost at once, he decided to let go and sprang onto William's back, digging his claws in. Then he jumped off, boxing the boy's ears, before sitting down politely.

"Ouch!" William rubbed his ears and Beelzebub twitched his tail as they pretended to ignore each other.

Seeing that the newly named Beelzebub was occupied with

William, Clara hurried silently for the attic, eyeing him surreptitiously as she glided past.

"Well, I bid you goodnight, gentlemen," she said quietly, hitching her skirts up with one hand and holding the candle in the other. She trod swiftly up the ladder-like stairs to the upper floor. Finally, the day before leaving, she had become used to the precarious climb to the room that was now her own quarters.

* * * *

With the daylight completely gone, the menfolk busied themselves for bed too. Jack pulled out the little truckle bed for William. When they pulled the basin of warm water from beside the dying fire, Beelzebub stood up and cocked his head. At the sound of sloshing water, he shot across to the farthermost side of the room, almost falling down the stairs. Quickly regaining his composure, however, he sat demurely, staring at them through wary, half-closed eyes as they stripped and washed, his kinky tail flicking silently from side to side. But as the men settled down to the gentle sounds of Clara's movements in the room above them, Beelzebub began meowing short, harsh calls and staring at the ladder leading to Clara's quarters. Jack and William eyed each other.

"Mayhap he longs to go upstairs," William said.

Jack smiled softly. "You go," he said. As the naked boy flung his sheets off and began padding to the door, he shook his head. "Put your smock back on, William! Good. Now see if he'll let you help him up." Then he added, "Go in gentle like, with a little knock. Do not barge in on Miss Clara!"

Nodding, William picked Beelzebub up. It took a good few seconds, even though he knew enough to secure the cat by placing his hand on the back of its neck first. Beelzebub twisted and squirmed and protested with vicious nips and scratches, but William was brave and persevering. At last he had a firm grip on the beast, even though his front claws were embedded in the boy's skull and his back claws hooked on his shoulder, and with his tail batting William's cheek, Beelzebub allowed himself to be carried up to the ladies' quarters. Jack laughed silently under his linen sheet at the entertainment.

William returned some minutes later and informed his master, "It was all right, I did not find Miss Clara undressing, sir, only saying her prayers."

In spite of his earlier laughter, Jack was kind enough to ask,

"Did the cat scratch you badly? Are you bleeding?"

* * * *

Although sleep came quickly and easily to Jack, his rest was fitful. He dreamt that he was having a fairly normal day, but all through the dream Dermot kept popping up, literally. Climbing out of the salt well while he was eating, sliding out from under the material he was cutting. Each visitation was more unnerving than the last. It culminated with Dermot climbing into his bed as he lay down to sleep. Jack tried to sit up, protesting, but Dermot had him pinned down, leaning on his chest, massaging his fingers in his flesh and murmuring throatily. Jack tried to cry out and fight the old man off, but he found he could not speak and he could not move. Dermot shoved his ugly face close to Jack's and grinned lustily, saying, "You're too tentative, far too tentative."

"Don't you mean sensitive?" Jack croaked, finding his tongue at last.

But Dermot ignored him and stared blissfully into middle space, still humming in that sickeningly suggestive tone. Jack felt cold with dread and horror as he tried in vain to struggle. Dermot's lurid humming grew deeper and stronger as his fingers continued their sensual, rhythmic massaging. Gripping and loosening, round and round. The intensity of this violation increased in parallel with Jack's mounting panic, until he awoke with an anguished cry as, finally, he managed to sit up. Back in the real waking world.

Beelzebub slid off of his chest as he rose—"Why, it's the blessed cat!—and rolled over and off the bed with a disgruntled bleat. He shook himself and glared accusingly through the gloom of the shuttered room at Jack. Jack glared back at him with matching aggression, until Beelzebub turned haughtily, his tail rising in the air. He paused like that for a moment, as though deliberately trying to offend Jack by displaying the worst possible view of him, before stalking across the room to the staircase. He climbed slowly and deliberately up to Clara's room.

"You evil, lying spawn of Satan," Jack breathed, staring after the cat, "you could climb that by yourself all along!" Then, realizing it was the break of day, he thought of the fabric waiting downstairs to be cut. Although it was a holy day—Saint Toole's parade day—and therefore not a day of work, he was anxious to keep ahead of his workload. There was light and time enough to cut the pieces so they'd be ready to begin sewing the next day. With renewed optimism, he swung his feet round to get out of bed as he grabbed his smock. His bare feet touched something small and soft and wet. Peering down at the floor, he guessed, rather than knew, what it was. Gingerly tiptoeing across to the windows, he flung the shutters open. The sky was still dark up high, but the rooftops opposite were glinting red and golden with the rising sun, and a gentle light fingered its way into the room. But he saw none of the dawn's beauty as he trod back to take a better look at his bedside. There was a little row of livers. Three tiny little livers.

"Good work, cat!" Jack snarled.

Chapter Sixteen

Clara's personal belongings lay folded in a neat pile on her bed. Apart from her basic clothes were six ribbons for her hair and her comb. And the yellow leather belt, purse and sheath, still wrapped up in the linen cloth. She wasn't sure if she should bother to take them on her pilgrimage to the Convent of Saint Alba's Jawbone. She would enter it with only the clothes on her back, saving that purse of money with which to buy her position, the money from her father. He had so much wanted to be rid of her that he'd parted with that generous amount in an instant.

Clara had already spent her first waking hour in prayer and meditation, seeking comfort and communion with God, but had found none. Indeed, she felt quite disgruntled and miserably heartsore. Perhaps extra prayer had an adverse effect on her, rather than lifting her spirits up. She would enter into the convent and pray and pray until she became a miserable, acidic little nun, shriveled up inside and out with bitterness. She'd eventually die lonely, and her earthbound spirit would haunt the cloister for hundreds of years—perhaps it would be known as 'the black nun, forewarning death and disaster.

With a heavy sigh, and another attempted smile—at Beelzebub's gymnastic feats as he washed himself—Clara crossed to the window and stared out at the new day. The sun was climbing up, trying to see its way through the thin, scattered clouds, glinting around their edges and bleaching the city walls. A pigeon perched boldly on the rooftop of the opposite house, cooed encouragingly to the sun before losing its nerve and taking flight. The scratching of its claws on the tiles and the frantic beating of its wings were clear, the street was that quiet.

But there was a tingle in the air, a sense of expectancy. A trio of children darted down the street, and a door slammed. A mother called and footsteps echoed hurriedly. Clara tried to etch the pattern of the rooftops and every soulful window on her mind's eye. Something to savor later—when cloistered all alone in her little cell, far from the distractions of the world, she would conjure up this sight and remember her time in Godwick, with Jack.

Naturally, she'd exclude from her fond memories the faint smell of rot that wafted up on the gusty hints of breeze. And so too the sound of Beelzebub licking away at his privates.

"For pity's sake, Beelzebub," she said, looking down at the cat as she passed him, "will you not allow me to indulge in a sentimental moment?"

He boxed her skirts in reply and she bent down, gently scratching the top of his head. She would have picked him up onto her lap and laid a tearful cheek upon his soft fur, but he maneuvered into an attack position and caught her hand and bit it. Although initially she tensed and pulled back, she finally relaxed and let him chew on her limp fingers.

"Oh, Beelzebub, why does Jack love Ingrid so? Why does she get to choose between two men, while I have none?" Clara mused on that for a moment before concluding, "I suppose I should see it as a sign that God is keeping me for himself and be delighted at such an honor. But it feels more like purgatory...no, like Hell... this vow of silence, being cloistered away...all that will be the easy task. 'Tis not being with Jack that will turn each moment of every day into Hell's agony."

Beelzebub froze and narrowed his eyes as his ears twitched. He was listening, but not to Clara. Loosening his grip on her hand, he twisted round and abandoned her.

"Hey, cat! Come back!"

Staring intently, Beelzebub began to stalk toward the crib, his muscles rippling with each silent step, his ears picking up a tiny scuffling that hers were deaf to.

"I am speaking to...oh, never mind!" Clara said. She gazed unseeingly toward the cat's destination before rising and making for the stairs.

By the time she reached the solar, she had managed to put on a half-baked smile.

"Good...oh. Where is everybody?" she muttered, looking around. The shutters were opened, the fire kindled, and a bowl of dough was rising in its warm glow. The beds were made, with the truckle bed tucked neatly back under the larger one. Clara's shoulders dropped under another sigh. She checked the chamber pot to see if the lousiest task had been left for her, but that too was done. She looked about, trying to ignore the dull ache in her throat, the tide of anguish rising in her chest.

Although one of the pipkins was already missing, gone to be filled with the day's ale, she took the other one and made for the stairs. If Jack heard her coming down to the shop, he pretended he did not. She gave him the benefit of the doubt; he was cutting out at the workbench, although instead of his working smock he was dressed in his Sunday best, ready for the parade. She watched him work for a moment, as she had done—was it just a few days ago? It seemed like years.

He straightened up and turned around, setting her heart on fire. He nodded in greeting, and she put on what she hoped passed for a smile.

"I have already sent William out," Jack said, indicating the jug in her hands with his scissors. It was a meaningless gesture, but she couldn't help wondering if there was some aggression in his movements. She looked down and realized she was clutching the jug to her chest, but she found she could not loosen her grip on it.

"Is it later than I thought? Have I overslept?" she asked. Her voice crackled like dry, autumn leaves.

Jack had turned away from her, looking back at his work, studying it from this angle and that.

"I was up early," he said. "I wished to get this cut out before... before we all go...out. And I sent William to get the ale early for the same reason."

Clara nodded, searched for something to say, but found nothing. She longed to move toward him—to fling herself into his arms—but she couldn't take a step forward. Jack began cutting again. The noise of the scissors seemed louder, coarser than usual, as it bit its way through the fabric. Clara shut her eyes tight, telling herself that she was listening one last time to the rhythmic crunch...crunch...crunch of the scissors. Telling herself that there was no lump burning in her throat.

At last she turned to go back upstairs, but before she had reached the bottom step, the shop door burst open, and William, also in smart attire, leaped in, ale sloshing out of the pipkin in his hand.

"Master! Master Jack! They're coming," he gabbled breathlessly, his face flushed and his hair ruffled. Jack and Clara focused on him instantly. Taking a deep, slowing breath, he went on, "The soldiers on the lookout have seen the Saint Alba's pilgrim procession. They are coming!"

Jack turned his attention to Clara. Despite the pang in her chest as his eyes met hers, she said calmly, "I am ready." In the silence that followed she slowly ran her tongue over the roof of her mouth, and felt the bump.

William said in a tiny voice, "But they are far off, yet, Miss Clara. You have an hour, perhaps, before they reach the gates."

Clara smiled and nodded, stepped forward and took the pipkin from his hands. "Good! Then we've time to eat breakfast first. One last..." Her voice trailed off, as she took more care than was necessary with the jug. "I'll make the crumpets."

Jack said, "We have some honey to go with them."

"Yippee!" William said.

* * * *

With the cutting finished and the downstairs shutters pulled closed, they all assembled upstairs to the aromatic smell of freshly cooked griddle cakes. William prattled on endlessly about nothing in particular as he trickled far too much honey over his cakes and licked his sticky fingers. Jack made no move to correct him, if, indeed, he even noticed. He seemed to spend forever over one griddle cake, and showed no delight at the tasty treat. Likewise Clara, tending to stare vacantly ahead, pushed her morsel about on her board, taking tiny nibbles and smiling absently at William from time to time. The pile of crumpets, instead of diminishing, only grew cold.

Jack shifted and fidgeted until Clara began to suspect he may have an infestation of fleas. Then, somehow, his gaze seemed to fix on Clara, and he grew still, like someone readying himself for a high dive.

"Clara...?" he began, but he never finished. He was interrupted by a flurry of knocking downstairs. For a moment they simply looked at each other. Clara stood up, and then Jack and William.

"Surely they're not at the door?" she whispered and hung back, allowing the men to go down first.

Slowly, she began to cross to the stairs that led up to her "quarters" where her purse of coins waited. But she had not taken more than two steps when she stopped and turned, listening

She heard a familiar woman's voice talking with Jack—and William exclaiming, "We've got a cat! His name is Beelzebub because he's so wicked!"

Clara hurried down to the shop, to confirm her suspicions. There, in the doorway, was Ingrid, beautifully flushed and wearing the nice new sleeves that Jack had made her.

"Come on, Clara!" Ingrid called cheerfully, "The Saint Alba's Jawbone Pilgrim parade is entering the gates. They'll follow the route around the market bell, and you can join with them when they get to the common."

Clara nodded. "I shall need my dowry," she said, turning to go back up the stairs.

As a thought struck her, she paused to face Ingrid. "You look well. So bright and cheerful...as though something good has happened..." She waited, her eyebrows raised. Had Ingrid already received a certain proposal?

Ingrid threw her head back and laughed. "Lord, no! 'Tis merely the chase—the excitement of running here, and hearing along the way news that your parade was near too." She turned her sparkling eyes on Jack. "Father John sent me to hurry you along, Jack!" She grinned, slipping her smooth, white hand into the crook of his arm.

Clara whipped round and started up the stairs again, saying, "I shall not be long."

The others crowded after her, blocking up the landing at the top of the first flight, William urging Ingrid to come up and see their new cat. Seeing the crumpets, she squeezed past William, saying, "Oh, I cannot ignore these crumpets!" She helped herself to one, dripping honey over it, and ate it ravenously. Honey trickled off of it, threatening to spoil her nice new sleeves. "I was too busy this morning to break my fast," she explained thickly, and laughed, eyeing Jack as she licked her sticky fingers suggestively.

Clara hauled herself up the higher steps and into her room. Beelzebub was crouching over something near the windowsill, and he shifted and glared at her as she came in. His tail flicked from side to side, and he bared his teeth in greeting. Quite forgetting why she had come up to the room in the first place, Clara, a true woman, leapt at the chance to talk about her feelings. Any pair of ears would do, and Beelzebub had excellent ears that twitched and maneuvered in response to her words.

"I cannot believe 'tis really, truly happening, Beelzebub!" she said, her voice hushed and intense. "That is, all this time, I believed—deep in my heart—I hoped that somehow, something would come about and I would...find myself with Jack. But not with *her* down there, flirting away like there's no tomorrow," she went on, pacing up and down, gesticulating as she counted all Ingrid's attributes, "swanning about in those sleeves he made her, and looking exquisite. With lustrous hair, big, sparkling blue eyes; full, red lips, cute little itty bitty nose, rosy cheeks, perfect figure. Oh! Does it never end!" She bent down low to engage her audience, unaware of his flattened ears, narrowed eyes and restless tail. "And she will receive two proposals before the day's out. *Two!* And me? I am to be marched off to become a nun. I shan't, I fear, make a good nun. I lust over *you know who* too much. I cannot look at him without drooling!" She sat down heavily on the foot of the bed, put her head in her hands and uttered a forlorn little groan. Beelzebub took the opportunity of her covered eyes to grab his midmorning snack, and, as any true lad would do, he hurried away.

"Oh," Clara whimpered, slowly lifting her horror-stricken face up to the light of the window, "I'm becoming like Dermot!"

* * * *

Ingrid, meanwhile, was licking the last of the honey off of her fingers. She tilted her pretty head just so, looking up through her long lashes at Jack, as she drew her pinkie finger slowly out of her mouth. Then she held out her hand to him. "Come on, Jack," she purred, "time to join the Saint Toole's parade."

He gulped and looked about, this way and that. "So soon? We have not finished breakfast. Mayhap we should say goodbye to Clara."

As he spoke Beelzebub dropped lightly from the last step, a limp mouse hanging from his jaws. Eyeing the party warily, he padded across to the foot of the bed. Jack watched him with equal suspicion, and William began telling Ingrid to "feast her eyes on this beast!" but she hardly seemed aware of him at all. She swept an empty bowl off of the nearest chest and placed it over the crumpets. "There!" she said. "You, Jack, have the honor of leading the parade with the reliquary, remember? Father John sent me here to fetch you. He awaits you there; now hasten!"

She stepped toward him with an outstretched hand as she spoke, but Jack stepped out of her way. Beelzebub had just jumped on the bed with his catch, and was obviously settling down to eat it there.

"Nay, out!" Jack snapped, causing a moment of confusion for poor Ingrid. "Not in here!" He tried to sweep the cat off of the bed. But Beelzebub's razor talon-encrusted paw shot at Jack's approaching hand like a bolt from a crossbow and caught him a blood-letting swipe, accompanied by vicious spitting and snarling and the other armed paw. Jack jumped back, recovered quickly and tried to approach the cat again. William paled as he watched from the doorway.

"No! Get off!" Jack ordered sternly, pointing his finger.

"PSSsss...NEOOOOW...Psssfffft!" Beelzebub shot back with a second clawed attack at Jack's hand. He kept out of the way, though, and tried to shoo Beelzebub off again.

"Oh, Jack!" Ingrid laughed. "He is not a customer; you need not be so kind!" Approaching the cat from behind as she spoke, she gave it a hearty shove. He shot off the bed in a firework of spat abuse, and his prey went flying too, landing just behind him. Beelzebub shrieked and attacked the air around him, lunged at Ingrid, but broke off halfway to flip back and retrieve his little dead mouse. He gave it a quick and nasty beating before skidding under the bed with it.

Even Ingrid paused for thought. But not for long, as she soon caught Jack's arm and grabbed William by the collar.

"That's settled then. Come, hasten yourselves, we are late!" She dragged them downstairs. "Oh, he's a splendid cat, William!

"But, Clara..." the boy began.

"We haven't said goodbye properly," Jack said, looking back.

"Clara does not wish it!" Ingrid insisted sharply and added that they were bound to bump into her as the two parades passed each other. "You can say farewell then," she finished, pulling the front door shut and herding the fellows down the street.

Clara, hearing the commotion, roused herself from her pit of despair with another sigh. She picked up the purse of money and with numerous backward glances at her possessions laid out on her bed, came down to the solar. She was just in time to hear the scuffle of feet downstairs.

"Are you all in the shop?" she asked. Her only answer was the slamming of the front door.

She stood still, listening for signs of their presence, but all she could hear was the crunching of little bones under the bed. She went downstairs to investigate, but no one was there. The shutter was closed and the shop was very dim, but she could see the cut-out surcoat Jack had worked on earlier laid neatly on the workbench, along with the scissors and a measuring stick. There was the bale of linen arrived yesterday, and there was the stool Jack had brought down from the solar. And an empty ale mug, she should move it; Jack didn't like untidiness in the shop. And here was where he'd stood as he haggled with a customer over the price of a russet kirtle, and there Clara had argued with him about yet another purchase of Mother Huckle's soap, and there was the doorway where she'd seen him with Ingrid, trying on her new sleeves...

"I'll just see myself out, then, shall I?" she said to the empty room, and she picked up the tankard, holding it to her cheek for a moment, thinking how Jack had held it in his hands and put it to his lips.

"Oh, this is ridiculous!" she cried, catching herself. And she stomped upstairs and plonked it down on the trestle table, still left out from their earlier meal.

"Goodbye, room," she said lamely. Again, a faint crunching was her only reply. "Goodbye, Beelzebub, wherever you are!"

Chapter Seventeen

Standing in the west transept of Saint Toole's Church, Jack endured two unpleasant factors, the first being the curate and the second the curate's assistant. They were openly snubbing him, looking him up and down but refusing to look him in the eye. They had given him only the barest, the haughtiest nod in greeting. When he, William and Ingrid had arrived, hurrying along the seemingly endless length of the knave, Father John had met them and led them to join the curate and the curate's assistant, and an entourage of altar boys and monks, ready for the parade. They were dressed in clean cassocks, and the eldest of the boys was helping the curate prepare the incense burner. The curate's assistant had hold of the replica of Saint Toole's hand. Father John took one look at Jack's scratched hand and tutted.

"Bathe that clean with some lavender water!"

"Nay, 'tis fine," Jack said, in hushed tones that hissed around the cavernous structure, "they are only from a cat."

"We cannot have you bleeding on the hand," Father John said. He was accustomed to the grandeur of the building and spoke quite loudly, his voice bounding off the great stone pillars and arches, drifting into the knave, where the first of the parishioners gathered for the march. He signaled irritably at the curate's assistant, who reluctantly let go of the hand, gave Jack a withering look and went off with little mincing steps.

"What is the hour? I fear we are late," Father John said, pushing the altar boys here and there, jostling them into their correct positions. William, who had gravitated to the reliquary and was staring at it intently, was shoved into place just behind the spot where Jack was intended to walk.

The curate's assistant reappeared with a bowl of lavender water and a square cloth of linen. Ingrid stepped forward and snatched them from him, quickly took over the wiping of Jack's bleeding hand.

"Master Jack was attacked by our cat!" William explained. The curate and the curate's assistant sniggered, and the altar boys copied their example. Father John rolled his eyes.

"He is a wild and vicious beast," William explained, "And he had a mind to eat this rat on Master Jack's bed, but when Master went to shoo him off, he attacked him." No one said anything, and after a little consideration William added, "We call him Beelzebub." The silence following that was even heavier than the last.

"Miss Ingrid pushed him off, though—the cat," he said.

Again the curate and the curate's assistant sniggered. Father John rocked on his heels, listening to the growing shuffling and muttering that drifted in from the nave. He walked across and peeked out of the door, and William scampered after him to look out too. The curate and the curate's assistant gave each other knowing looks.

As Ingrid dabbed at Jack's hand far longer than was necessary, she chided him coyly about his lost battle with the cat.

"You need to be firm with that cat, Jack. All this 'if it does not offend you' and 'if you are agreed' approach is good for customers, but 'tisn't very masterful, Jack," she whispered. "Do not be shy in...asking for what you want. Or," she dipped her head and eyed him through her lashes, "someone else may take it...Or her," she mouthed, "... right before your very eyes!"

Jack stared sullenly at her, a slight frown beginning to play on his brow. Luckily he was saved from having to answer her riddle of a statement by Father John, who hurriedly crossed over to them; his vestments flapped about him, giving the impression of an agitated hen.

He peered at Jack's hand. "Come along, wench; how long do you need to wipe the blood from a scratch?"

"It was dried and encrusted," Ingrid mumbled.

"Well, 'tis fine now," Father John said. He gave Jack's wound a slap fit to set the bleeding off again. "Let us be gone! There is a crowd out yonder, all ready to go. And I want us to get to the common before the Saint Alba's parade does. Last year they trod it into a right mire! We had to wade through a pit of mud, and one of my shoes was sucked off."

The altar boys hastily inspected their cassocks, and two of the boys squabbled in silent gestures over who would hold the vessel of holy water. The curate and his assistant took the incense burner and the holy water from the boys, who had to be content with carrying the two accompanying banners, while two monks had hold of the reliquary. It was an ornate box of silver plated engravings, and it lay on a litter draped with a velvet cloth.

"I never did find my shoe again," Father John confided in Ingrid, and then without pausing for breath, he burst into a Latin prayer song, which was immediately picked up by his curates, the altar boys and the monks. The parade had begun. Two monks waving an incense burner, followed by two banner-holding altar boys stepped out of the transept and into the knave. They were followed by the reliquary, carried like a king on a litter, and after the holy relic, came Father John, the curate and the curate's assistant, with the incense and holy water, followed by Jack with the replica hand on its pike, Ingrid, William and a tail of altar boys. They proceeded down the knave, with the parishioners parting in biblical fashion before them and then following in their wake, trying to catch a few drops of holy water, which the curate sprinkled with rhythmic, sweeping motions of his arm. Their voices, chanting in Latin verse, and the curling smoke of the incense rose heavenward. It brought tears to some followers' eyes. William certainly seemed to be caught up in the mood; he looked up at the vaulted ceiling, whispering a prayer of his own. However, this action caused him to bump into the curate's assistant, who whipped round and scowled at him, without missing a beat or a word of the verse.

"Are you well, lad?" Jack whispered. "Is that smoke in your eyes, or were you talking in tongues?"

His attempt at humor was lost on William, who answered through the side of his mouth, "I was praying that Miss Clara's prayer be answered."

Jack glanced around; then, still trying to shuffle forward in the parade, he bent down close to William and asked, "What prayer?"

William shrugged. "You remember, Master Jack? When I took Beelzebub up to her, she was praying. She was saying..."

But William didn't get to finish his sentence. As he and Jack consorted, the replica hand, being top heavy, swung forward and bumped the curate's assistant on the back of the head. He whipped round angrily and glared at the pair.

"*Shh*!" he hissed, with more ferocity than even Beelzebub could summon. Jack and William behaved themselves instantly, adopting overly rigid stances and faces of wooden gravity. Their lips moved in their mumbled attempts to join in the Latin prayer.

Chapter Eighteen

Clara stepped out into the empty street; with everyone gone to join the parade, it was a street as silent as a stillborn child, the shops shuttered, the houses empty. Litter dotted the gutters, and a broken basket lay in the middle of the street. Somewhere a shop sign creaked on its chain. Thanks to the stiff breeze, she was not too hot with her cloak draped over her plainest woolen surcoat. The extra changes of clothes she had felt she could not leave her father's house without now lay abandoned in Jack's house. She took one last look at the closed door, then turned her back on it. She thought of the advice given to the apostles—to wipe the dust off their sandals as they left hostile towns. She was wearing shoes, but, she thought, the biblical reference was there nevertheless. Yes, Godwick was all part of the past now—her time spent with Jack—done and dusted. God had not sent her a miraculous event to deliver her from her fate, despite her feverish prayers. Prayers she'd managed despite being interrupted by a certain apprentice boy delivering a cat to her room.

It was the life of a cloistered and silent nun for her. She thought, rather irritably, how grand it would have been if she had also, like Jack, been sent an escort to where she was to join up with the pilgrims of Saint Alba and her fused Jawbone. With a sigh, and the breeze tugging vainly at her tightly secured wimple, Clara's life of chastity was beginning right then, as she turned slowly and crossed the street to make her way to the city gates.

She had not gone two yards when Mrs. Gimmer, the tailor's wife—from the house she had trespassed into—came out of her front door. Clara froze as their eyes met, a wave of cold horror immediately following the initial ripple of surprise she felt at finding another living person still in the street. The woman recognized her at once.

"Ah! You!" she called, raising her hand and hurrying to meet Clara. "I know you!" Mrs. Gimmer went on, "You're the wench with Jack Paisley—the new tailor opposite." She pointed to Jack's house as Clara nodded, the blood draining from her face.

"Horrid, cursed house!" Mrs. Gimmer said, lowering her voice,

"It's haunted!"

"Haunted?" Clara squeaked.

Mrs. Gimmer nodded and said, "If the living, breathing Dermot wasn't bad enough, his ghost is worse. Have you not felt his presence since his demise?"

Clara glanced to the side before replying, "Er...I'm still recovering from the *living* Dermot." At least she spoke the truth, even though it was a little over the top.

"Yes! Horrible, lecherous man," Mrs. Gimmer said, and she peered into Clara's eyes. "How you managed to escape being molested is a wonder."

"Jack was very protective towards me," Clara replied, her voice cracking.

Mrs. Gimmer grasped Clara's arm in a tight, motherly clench. "I know, poor you! Then, no sooner was Dermot gone when such banging and scratchings began that Jack, thinking he had rats, hurriedly sought a cat."

"Well, there was always evidence of rats..." Clara admitted truthfully, but Mrs. Gimmer wasn't going to be diverted from her tale.

"And breathing," she embellished expressively, "vile, heavy breathing. Why, 'tis no wonder you are fleeing that house to join a convent."

Clara managed a wan smile.

"And just the other day," Mrs. Gimmer added, with a slow, knowing nod, "I had a terrifying encounter with Dermot's ghost."

Clara's eyebrows arched as she bit her bottom lip.

Mrs. Gimmer found this was sufficient encouragement to continue her tale of horror. "I was sitting on my bed, as quiet and calm as can be, and only scantily dressed in my chemise, recovering from one of my headaches, you understand. And there I was, in my underwear, when a ghastly figure floated in through the window, from your side of the street. A robed, ghostly creature!"

Clara swallowed and blinked. "Didn't you recognize...who it was?" she asked.

"Dermot!" the woman hissed, "Dermot, straight from the bowels of hell! Dressed in burial robes he was, and reeking of brimstone."

"No...but," Clara, still frowning, looked appealingly at Mrs. Gimmer. "*Reeking?* Are you sure?" she asked.

Her neighbor nodded enthusiastically and continued, "Then he lunged for me—ooh! I felt his lecherous, rotting fingers brush past my neck as I fled from the room..."

"I...he..." Clara began.

"So ragged was his breathing, so evil were his muttered obscenities."

"Nay! Apologies!" Clara cried, her face reddening, "He was apologizing...er...for his lechery...surely?" She put her hand over her mouth.

Mrs. Gimmer shook her head firmly. "No. It was obscenities. Too disgusting to tell a young maid like yourself." And she added as an afterthought, "I felt him brush past me. I was chilled to the bone for hours afterwards. "

Clara chewed on her bottom lip, her brow furrowed as she stared at Mrs. Gimmer. Then she sighed and shook her head sympathetically. "The bastard!"

Mrs. Gimmer nodded again and continued her tale. "My husband and I gave chase, believing at first that he was an intruder, a thief. And a soldier joined in the chase, but by the mysterious way he disappeared, in a swirling mist down Whores' Alley—*Whores' Alley*, mind you—the men knew, as I insisted from the start, that he was a ghost. The ghost of Dermot. Ooh, Miss Clara! You are right to abandon that house of evil. I told Jack to get the house blessed..."

"And so he did!"

"A sprinkling and a blessing, that's what that house needs!"

Clara swallowed. "Absolutely," she agreed, "be sure to tell Jack, for me."

"I will, but now I must depart. The parade is already starting, and you had better head for the gates! Sorry, my dear, I cannot follow you on your pilgrimage parade—I have to support Saint Toole!"

At last, Mrs. Gimmer turned to go, but just as soon, she turned back and added, "God bless you!" and she directed Clara down what she thought was the best route to the gates, then hurried off toward the church.

As Clara wound her way through alleys and streets to the gates, she kept her mind on Mrs. Gimmer, which was easier to bear than any of the other options she could have dwelt on. As she concluded that for someone who was afraid of ghosts, Mrs. Gimmer was spooky herself, Clara turned a corner to find herself looking up at the gate house. The streets were busy here.

Beggars crawled along the gutters, ready to snatch up what blessings and morsels might be cast their way by the richer flock from the castle end of town. And there they were, swanning about in their fine velvets and silks. Peddlers and jugglers added a splash of color and a dash of effervescence to the milling crowds. A dog with a limp scuttled, hunchbacked and tail between its legs, out of a foot soldier's way. There was a stream of men-in-arms patrolling through the streets, watching from the city walls, while mounted knights in full regalia rode on prancing steeds.

It was out of this confusion of milling people and beasts waiting expectantly for the arrival of the pilgrims that Burke de Montfort rode up to Clara.

He greeted her eloquently. "Good day, fair maiden!" He flashed his customary smile and wink.

Eyeing him with the same desperation that a drowning man might consider a straw, Clara noticed that he had a dimple on his chin, and she noticed too how clean and newly shaved it was. She nodded and smiled demurely, in good fair maiden tradition, wishing she had let her hair out.

He leaned on the pommel and, letting his charming smile emanate down to her level, said, "Well, wish me luck!"

For a moment Clara stared up at him, her face still and wooden. "Ah!" she cried at last, then asked more carefully, "Then you have not yet...asked her...yet?"

"No! But I intend to—shortly. I have orders to mind the two parades and make sure they don't clash. Last year we all but had a riot, you know! My uncle has no wish for Godwick to be the cause of a full-scale peasant uprising. Anyhow, I am bound to spot my beloved Ingrid, and as soon as she sees me on my mount, I plan to gallop over to her, sweep her up onto the saddle and propose. Marriage, of course."

Clara's lips twitched. "How charming!"

"Exactly!"

"She shall not be able to offer the slightest resistance!" Clara grinned and cupped her hand over her mouth.

Burke colored boyishly. "Do you reckon so, too? What are my chances, would you say?"

Clara shrugged her shoulders and coughed. She thought he had at least a sporting chance, but knew that he would see that as too cruel. At last she decided that it would be safest to ask, "Do you know of any competition?"

Burke brushed a fly from his upper arm. "Nothing worth considering."

"Well, then, I should think your chances were very high. But

Ingrid is popular, and if you leave it too late, some other admirer..." Clara slid her tongue over the roof of her mouth and let her voice trail off meaningfully.

"No! Today is the day! And if any man stands in my way, I shall run him through with my sword!"

Clara clutched at her breast. "I beg you, don't..."

Burke threw back his head and laughed. "'Tis a jest!" He winked and spurred his horse on before pausing to call over his shoulder, "Well, see you anon! Wait! I shan't see you, shall I? Ah, well, God be with you!"

And he and his dimpled chin rode off, melting into the bustling crowd. Clara stood staring dismally ahead for a few moments, when Burke, having trotted his steed in a tight circle, appeared at her side again. Noisy though his mounted approach was, she still jumped when he leaned down and said, "They have arrived! Just coming through the gates—your Saint Alba's pilgrims!"

Clara followed the line his gloved hand pointed to. She forced an animated smile and an overzealous nod. "Ah, yes! Wonderful!" And stepping out, she readied herself to join the back of the procession.

Through the shadowy arch of the gate house walked the pilgrims of Saint Alba's Jawbone. It was gray upon gray upon gray. The towering stone walls, all grime stained at the bottom, rising up into the rippling gray eiderdown of sky. Even as the parade emerged from the shadowy arch of the gate house, in their somber procession, the wind slowly rolled a particularly dark, billowing carpet of cloud over the skies of Godwick.

The nuns and novices wore dark gray woven wool, and wimples tighter even than Clara's. Studying the little milk faces that peeped out of their gray encasements, she winced at the thought of the shaven heads beneath the linen and tweed. They all looked—not unhappy—but so very contained. No one ever rattled off like a bolting horse in that convent. No one was ever swept away on a tide of emotions. Even their laymen followers wore drab colors and clean slate faces.

The most animated thing in the parade was a glorified placard of Saint Alba's face. Held high between two painstakingly embroidered banners, it was a rather two-dimensional representation, cut from a light wood. It was delicately stained here and there with dull colors to emphasize features. It was a humble, simple piece of work, and therein was its beauty. As Clara's eyes lingered, it exuded an air of eeriness. Perhaps it was the way the jaw moved, with that stilted animation of crude puppetry. Up and down, as though singing with the procession, a monotonous chanted hymn of praise. Being women, mostly, the chorus of voices was high and thin. It was delicate, but with a hidden strength, like a silvery spider's web spreading out over the town. So light it was that the wind plucked the song up and tossed it about, and it drifted ahead of the procession in a hauntingly beautiful veil of sound. Clara strained to see the moving lips of the usually silent nuns. How they must look forward to the chance to sing and pray!

She realized there were more pilgrims than nuns as she pushed her way forward to approach one of the more welcoming nuns. After walking alongside the procession for a good few yards, she spotted an older nun, with what could be a twinkle in her eye. Clara drew up alongside her, and, clearing her throat, tapped the wide sleeve—yes, the fabric was indeed very rough. The old nun turned and met Clara's questioning gaze. She nodded demurely and didn't look away, studied Clara's face. Clara, looking back at the nun, searched for that warm flicker, that promise of kind acceptance. Twinkling or not, the nun's eyes, Clara concluded, were impenetrable. Indeed, they were the sort that bore into you in a benign way. Like a still pool in a cavern, it was hard to gauge their depth. She wasn't sure if they were hazel or just old and murky. The nun raised her eyebrows expectantly.

"Erm...Mother....Sister...ma'am," Clara said in fits and starts, her voice all weak and wispy, "I wish to join the convent of Saint Alba's Jawbone."

The old woman stared impassively at her for a moment. Her pale withered lips were a thin line in her wrinkled face. Then she nodded toward a clerical-looking man who stepped out of the belly of the parade quickly and silently. He was small boned and carried no extra weight. He was the sort of man who could pass as a woman with no more effort than slipping into a woman's garments. Clara got the impression he had been aware of her presence on the sidelines, aware of her intentions before she had even spoken, but she repeated her request to him.

His eyes creased at the corners as he delivered a drab smile. "My child, do you have any recommendation?" he asked.

Clara pulled her purse up, leaving it attached to her belt, and jingled it in front of him, emphasizing its weight by pushing it upward with the palm of her hand.

His smile broadened, and he patted her arm and said, "Come, join in the back of the line. Mother Superior will welcome you into the convent when we reach our destination."

"But...but how...I mean..."

"I will seek you out."

With that assurance, Clara found herself standing still as the parade and crowds pushed past and around her.

"Right," she said after some time. She could now make out the end of the procession, and as she stepped forward to join the more inner group of followers, she muttered to herself, "What I was asking, of course, was *how* would Mother Superior speak to me as such...or would he do all the talking for her? How does he know what she wishes to say? Does he read her thoughts, I wonder?"

Chapter Nineteen

It was good that the citizens of Godwick showed such ardent support for their patron saint, but the Saint Toole's parade, Jack thought, was verging on a sacrilegious farce. There was a buzz of anticipation, tinged with aggression that flicked through the air like lightning. It was no wonder that Lord de Montforte had ordered his men to keep the parade separate from the Saint Alba's pilgrim march. Their routes were planned quite carefully not to come into contact. Indeed, Jack was beginning to wonder if he'd manage to catch a glimpse of the Saint Alba's pilgrims parading at all, despite Ingrid assuring him that there was a fault in the plan of the routes. They were, she assured him, bound to come quite close at one point. That would have to do.

It seemed as though they'd been tramping through Godwick's streets for hours with no sign of the pilgrims, nor of Clara. He began to fret that he could have missed them altogether. Onlookers—seemingly the poorer sections of the town's population—constantly dogged his view, milled annoyingly around the streets, following the parades and no doubt ready to switch loyalties at the slightest whim.

Peddlers were blatantly selling their wares, and acrobats, minstrels and tricksters were all doing as much business as possible. The constant presence of military strength did nothing to deter them. When the occasional overzealous worshipper made a lunge at the reliquary in the hope of touching the casket that housed the real hand of Saint Toole, the soldiers grinned to one another rather than moving in to peel them off the core of the parade.

At each of these attacks the bearers and surrounding monks would knit themselves tightly around the casket for some time, sprinkling vast amounts of holy water at the crowd to placate them, and chanting with extra volume. But their tight formation would begin to drift as they proceeded, until the next lunge from the crowd brought them scuttling hurriedly back in, making the banner and replica hand sway violently.

This was an annoying distraction for Jack, who was trying to hold in his mind's eye a picture of Clara's face. But at last, as the market square came into view, he saw the tail end of the parading Saint Alba's pilgrims filing onto one of the side streets. He strained to see past the parading Saint Toole supporters and the visiting pilgrims. Just as he was squinting in the effort to pick out one woman who looked like she could be Clara, Ingrid nudged him from behind, shifting his line of vision.

She whispered in his ear, "There's the Saint Alba's parade and their upper-crust followers. Can you spot Clara?"

No, but he could have throttled Ingrid! He quelled his initial annoyance at her interruption and, hoping she was pointing her out to him, he peered into the street that had just swallowed the pilgrims up. His efforts caused him to let the replica hand tip forward on its pike. It was a cumbersome thing to carry because it was so dreadfully top heavy, and seemed to lurch to one or the other side—or back and forth—at the slightest provocation. In this instant, as Jack was not quick enough to save it from butting the curate's assistant in the back of the head. The curate's assistant whipped round and glared at Jack, tutting loudly. Jack grinned sheepishly, but the curate's assistant only scowled harder before turning his attention back to the reliquary with a haughty flick of his head.

Ingrid tugged at Jack's sleeve and giggled. "He shall never forgive you, Jack!"

Jack managed a sideways glance at her as he was swept up the street in the parade. The onlookers seemed to leer mockingly at him, dancing and diving to keep his view to the side streets blocked. The replica hand wobbled with alarming frequency as Jack strained to get a glimpse down each and every side street and even the narrow lanes that they passed. He tried to filter in all the distant sounds, listening through the Latin refrain of the Saint Toole's parade, in the hope that the wind might bring him a hint of women's voices in chorus.

As the parade and its followers marched through the next intersection, turning off the main street into a street that ran along the back of the market, their route took them past his own house. He stared up at the shuttered building for some sign of life, but it was as forlorn and still as all the other houses.

He turned to William. "Do tell, William, what was Clara's request, in her prayers?"

William frowned and answered after what seemed to be an age of a pause, "I cannot fully understand what she said, Master Jack. It sounded like a quote of some sort."

"What exactly did she say?" Jack asked.

"She said—" William began, but then he scratched his head and broke off. "Would it be right to tell?" he asked.

Jack leaned over to demand, as his master, that William tell him word for word what he had heard, but the replica hand plunged sideways into the crowd as he did so. A group of desperate followers, bent on touching the reliquary, surged forward, sending the altar boys and monks into a wobbly stagger. Recovering their balance, they shooed the crowd back, and Jack used the replica hand as a top-heavy lance to do his bit. That was a mistake.

The crowd, being denied their wish to touch the holy relic, contented themselves with getting a sample of the replica hand, and two of William's ribbon tendrils were torn off. It was as though Jack had dipped the hand into the dark waters of a school of frenzied cloth-eating monsters. The pike bobbled about furiously under the attack, but with William, the curate and the curate's assistant all pulling gallantly with Jack, they managed to regain a strong hold on the replica hand of Saint Toole. It looked more gruesomely tattered at the wrist end than ever, and the little finger was dangling loose, leaving a trail of sawdust to be trampled into the beaten earth street.

Father John, having been forced to stare in horror from the front of the reliquary at the masses mauling the replica, hissed furiously into a nearby altar boy's ear. Between verses of Latin, his angry message was being passed on to Jack's soon-to-be-burning ears.

Luckily for him, though, the crowd of onlookers calmed down naturally as the street narrowed and bent, forcing them to thin out and trail farther behind the procession.

"William, tell me what you heard Clara saying," Jack demanded as soon as he had a chance. "Tell me word for word!"

"All I heard was, '...if it be in your will, oh Lord, I pray Thou would take this cup from me,'" the boy replied.

Jack frowned and repeated absently to himself, "'Take this cup from me.'"

"If you do not know the words to this prayer," the curate's assistant hissed, having stolen up between Jack and William, "*be quiet!*"

His voice rose so loudly that he himself received several glares from his Latin-singing brothers.

As a red hue seeped into his face, he snarled, "And Father John says if you let the replica hand lean into the crowd one more time, the honor of bearing it shall be taken from you and given to someone more worthy!" He flared his nostrils and tossed his head as he rejoined his position in the chorus.

"Jack!" Ingrid chided, nudging him and making him stagger. As the replica hand dipped, shaven heads swung warningly in his direction, but as a knight rode in a bit too close, his horse drew their attention away from Jack's incompetence.

It was the sheriff, Burke de Montfort, peering into the heart of the parade, looking for someone in particular. As he neared, the marchers to all sides stepped politely out of the way of his horse's hooves. This caused a tailback to ripple unsteadily along the parade. Again the replica hand dipped, and the crowd lunged for it—but more cautiously this time. The sheriff galloped at once to the heart of the scuffle, and peasants scattered instantly. However, another tendril was now stuffed into someone's chemise.

As the parade recovered its balance they reached the main road again, and Jack saw that only one street down, the Saint Alba's pilgrims were once again filing off the main street and onto a side street. Jack calculated that they would be going down Bakers' Street. He strained to see Clara, thought he saw her and, shoving the replica hand at an unsuspecting William, waved frantically. But—if, indeed, it was her—her head was down and she was not looking his way.

The crowd roared as the replica hand swayed under the change of hands and swung down their way. More stitching popped, and the ring finger was lost. William stared tearfully at the battered hand, and the curate's assistant whipped round and snatched the pole. Jack, William and Ingrid were quickly and silently banished to the outer regions of the formal parade.

The stir in the crowd as this last incident took place caused the Saint Alba's lot to slow down and stare. Was Clara looking now? Jack strained on tiptoe to see, but Ingrid was waving her hand in the way, and Burke de Montforte and two of his men galloped between the two groups, completely obscuring Jack's view. If that were not enough, a troop of foot soldiers ran to form a line between them, and the Saint Toole's parade poured into another side street as, yet again, Jack felt the blow of being severed from the Saint Alba's pilgrims and Clara.

* * * *

Clara, stomping numbly onwards with the Saint Alba's pilgrims' parade, gradually became aware that she had a neighbor. As they left the main street and filed into a narrower side street, for what seemed like the umpteenth time, she turned to stare openly at a young woman of her own age group walking along beside her. She was shorter than Clara by a full head, and could justly be described as plump. She had a round face, peeking benignly out of her tight wimple. Her chubby fingers poked modestly from her long, wide sleeves. Her loose calico chemise billowed out of the deep armholes and puffed out of the low neckline of her serviceable onion-brown surcoat. Her rosy, fat cheeks, button nose and rosebud mouth gave her round face a kindly look, and her brown eyes glowed softly with placidity. Clara drew the conclusion that this timid young woman was the sort of person who could slip unnoticed into a room and stand right next to you for some time before you realized she was even there. And then she wouldn't take the slightest offence at your snobbery. Clara smiled at her, and she flushed and smiled back.

"You're not a nun of this order, are you?" Clara asked at length.

Her neighbor shook her head, keeping her eyes cast down.

"Do you intend to enter the convent?" Clara asked, feeling just a little twinge of happiness at the thought of joining the order with a potential friend.

The woman afforded her only the slightest nod, but at least she smiled demurely.

"I too!" Clara mouthed with such an animated nodding that she almost loosened her wimple. They were silent for a long time. Clara hoped that it was a companionable sort of silence. She tried to think of possible times they would have together in the convent and how close they would become. She tried to use that exercise to push back any thoughts of Jack.

But as their route took them back toward the main street, Clara gasped. All her reserve and fortitude fizzled away in a shower of sparks at what she saw. At the mere prospect of who was within the body of marchers slipping onto the high street, just as they were leaving it.

"I think I saw the other parade as we left the main street," Clara said.

Her neighbor frowned and glanced backwards.

"Have no fear—I do not believe we will bump into them," Clara said. "They were entering it as we were leaving it."

They walked in silence for a few yards before Clara said, "They are not bad at all, in truth. They are good, friendly folk. I know them quite well...some of them..." She sighed and slowly slid her scarred tongue over the roof of her mouth.

As there seemed to be no opening for more conversation, Clara busied herself with watching the nuns. She began to notice that what had initially seemed to be swipes at summer wasps and tweaking of wimples could be a code of communication. When a third nun brushed her right sleeve in exactly the same way as two others, Clara smiled wryly to herself. She tried to catch her neighbor's eye, but the young woman was staring intently straight ahead. Perhaps, Clara thought, she was coming to the very same conclusion that she herself was. It seemed that over the years, what started off amongst the nuns as a nod and a smile had advanced to the tapping of sleeves, pulling of wimples, and raising of eyebrows. And if the essence of the silent rule of the convent was essentially being ignored by the nuns in this way—well, she was willing to play along with it.

Clara found her steps growing lighter. She leaned over and tapped her neighbor. "I wonder if there is not some sort of communicating going on between the nuns—see! Hark, yonder!" She pointed to one nun in particular, who was nodding to a second nun nearby.

Clara's neighbor turned her head stiffly in an arch, slowly getting round to meeting her eye, and replied with only the faintest smile and slightest, nervous nod.

Clara returned the communication vigorously and grinned. She went on with more animation than usual, "Little signals! I dare say it shall not be so bad after all—the vow of silence. In essence, one has to say at some point, 'pass the salt, please!' I'll wager I could manage that...never talking...erm... Not that it's bad. Nay, 'tis a good thing, silence is. So much of what we say is...unnecessary. My father always says I talk too much...indeed I am quite a chatterbox when I get going....so this will be good for me. A good cure for my...my bad...my incessant...chatter..." She trailed off. Her neighbor's stare had turned from bland to reproachful.

Clara frowned and bit her lip. "I'm talking too much now, aren't I?"

Her neighbor blinked, put a finger on her lips, and applied another micro smile. Looking away, Clara sighed.

Chapter Twenty

"What ails you?" Ingrid enquired, giving Jack a nudge. "Surely you are not peeved about having the hand taken from you?"

Unaware that he was pursing his lips, that a frown etched his brow, Jack guffawed. "Nay, never!" In truth he was glad. He could speak much more freely, farther away from the reliquary.

"About it being damaged, then?" Ingrid pressed.

"No."

"I am," William murmured, very quietly, so no one heard him.

"Nay, 'tis Clara," Jack said. "She said, 'Take this cup from me.'"

Ingrid raised her eyebrows. "Well? Did you refuse? Did it become a clearing-up issue? Did you argue?"

Jack almost snapped at her. "Nay, woman! In her prayers!" He sighed and pinched the bridge of his nose before continuing more calmly, "'Tis a passage from the Crucifixion. When Jesus said those words to God, he was saying he would rather not go through with the Crucifixion, if he didn't have to."

"But Clara's not being crucified!" Ingrid said, all wide eyed.

"Nay, but I have in mind she means becoming a nun!"

"Of course she means to be a nun! She can barely wait, she is so eager!"

"William heard her praying..." he began, but Ingrid cut him off.

"There now! All this extra praying you overheard is a sample of how devout Clara is. She has certainly been *called*, Jack. Clara has got to go!"

Jack gave her a sideways glance and, shrugging, let the subject drop. But the thickening clouds echoed his sullen scowl, and they continued in silence for some time.

The route of the Saint Toole's parade took them round the inside of the city wall at that point, and it became apparent that the duck pond on the common would be their next landmark. Jack knew that after rounding the pond, the parade would march back up the length of the High Street, to the church where it began. He thought they might just see the Saint Alba pilgrims again. One last time.

"Jack! Jack!" Ingrid tugged like a child at his sleeve. "I think Sheriff Burke is following me!"

"He is following the parade," he replied flatly, "he and his men."

"But he is staring this way. I have an inkling he's looking at me!"

Jack glanced over his shoulder. "Well, wave to him, then. Greet him!"

But whether Ingrid was about to argue with Jack or to follow his suggestion, no one would know, because at that point a member of the crowd following the parade lunged at the new bearer of the replica hand, and a frantic tussle ensued. Burke spurred his steed to a gallop while some foot soldiers ran to the trouble spot, but for a few desperate moments, they seemed only to add to the aggression and confusion. But at last the hand triumphantly rose upwards, battered but intact. The thumb had been ripped off, and now only the index and middle fingers remained. And the parade was tramping through another trail of spilled sawdust that had been used to thicken up the hand.

William's eyes glistened, and his face puckered up. But he swallowed hard. "At least the stumps look as though the hand's fingers are folded down, rather than missing."

"Mm," Jack said, staring at the hand ahead of them. "Therein lies a problem, methinks."

Ingrid giggled. "It does indeed look rude!" And after a while she added, "Let us hope the Saint Alba tribe are too pure of heart to see the vulgarity in its gesture."

* * * *

Clara, meanwhile, sighed and wished she were able to catch just one last glimpse of Jack in his parade. She began to strain at every corner, each time their path crossed another, in the hopes of spotting the Saint Toole's parade. And Jack. Godwick had never seemed so large, the streets so endless, the crowds so full as they did that day. People milled around the pilgrims constantly—and this was supposedly the smaller, richer community. The very poor followed them like ravished pilot fish while the entertainers pranced about like tropical fish, hoping for a reward to be tossed their way.

Clara found one joker in particular very annoying. He was of a similar build to Jack and of the same coloring. She kept thinking he was Jack flitting through the throngs, coming toward her to fetch her back. But it never turned out to be her love. Each time she stared at the man, hoping it was indeed Jack, the grinning joker pushed his leering face toward her, thinking she was about to toss a grout his way.

And if this teasing were not agonizing enough, she had to endure it all in silence. She was not to utter a single word of exasperation, not one word of lament to ease her angst. She longed to ask her so-called new friend and neighbor if she had received some sort of preparatory lessons in silence. And if so, if such training did exist, why hadn't she known about it? Why had no one—not least of all, Jack—told her? Things hardly seemed fair. Her neighbor was undoubtedly made for a silent order and therefore didn't need any tutoring in that field. Whereas she, Clara, who had been banished from home because of her wagging tongue, obviously needed urgent assistance. And plenty of it!

Casting her focus out, beyond her fellow pilgrims, Clara noticed that soldiers were tailing the parade. Were they there for protection, or to prevent potential novices in the throes of second thoughts from bolting to freedom? Or deflecting to the other parade? She knew she was being ridiculous, but keeping her thoughts tucked away in her head seemed only to get them all tangled up.

Would they stumble upon the Saint Toole parade again, glimpse it heading down another alley? Clara sighed; well, that seemed unlikely, as they were obviously making for the common and it's lovely little duck pond. She assumed they'd leave the city from the nearest gate, as by now they had surely wound their way through the whole of the town.

But then, oh joy! As the pilgrims filed out of a street that ran alongside the wall and out onto the common, Clara's heart leapt and she put a hand to her mouth to stifle a cry. There, approaching the duck pond from the opposite side of the common was the Saint Toole's parade. She strained at once to spot Jack, but it was difficult to see past Saint Alba's own supporters, let alone through the Saint Toole's faithful followers. Besides, at first it was not possible to recognize individual faces from the initial distance between the two parades, but Clara could not bring herself to stop looking—searching—for that one special smile. She did not notice that the Saint Alba's pilgrims had stopped until she bumped into the person in front of her; they had, as one body, hesitated at the sight of the Saint Toole's parade.

Clara was glad of the chance to stare at the group on the other side of the pond. She focused on the banner and the replica hand, sure that was where she would spot Jack. Just as she picked out the top of what she thought was his hood, and his hand holding the pole of the replica hand, the pilgrims started walking again, and her view was instantly blocked.

As they reached the narrowest part of the pond, the point at which the two teams came the closest to each other, the two groups stood still once again, for an instant, eyeing each other out. The sky seemed grayer and darker than ever. The wind held its breath as lightning zipped across the endless roll of cloud; then the wind resumed, buffeting the town with renewed vigor.

Clara looked across the rippling water and wondered how deep the duck pond was. She toyed with the idea of breaking free and wading to the other side. With gusts of wind tugging at her skirts, she eyed her fellow pilgrims, aware that all members of both parties were distracted by the presence of the other. The knight's horses whinnied and pawed at the ground. Another moment of still silence dropped over the common, and then giggling began to ripple through the Saint Alba's pilgrims.

Clara's heart sank as, absently, she cupped one of her cheeks. The Saint Toole's replica hand—that which William and Jack and even she herself had stitched—now looked deformed. It was somehow tattier, decidedly thinner. Then, she realized, with a gasp, that most of its fingers were missing! The stumpy wounds of the missing digits seemed like they were merely folded, not gone, and her eyes bulged as she interpreted the gesture it was apparently making with its two remaining fingers.

Surely, she thought, the Saint Toole's parade had not deliberately manipulated the hand into pulling such a crude sign. By the air of mortification emanating across the choppy water, she concluded not. She was torn between feeling relieved that the Saint Alba's group were not taking the involuntary gesture to heart, and annoyed at them for laughing at the Saint Toole's parade's misfortune.

Hissing whispers mingled with the giggling, and above that Clara heard a barked order: "Move along!"

It was probably one of the knights. Yet the command went ignored, blown away on the wind, along with the muted cackling of the Saint Alba's group.

"I beg you not to laugh, 'twould be unkind!" Clara muttered, scowling unheeded at the people around her. She squirmed as she noticed the look of disgust on her neighbor's podgy face, and she said, "They don't mean it. Something's happened to it."

Her neighbor sniffed, a slight smile tugging at her lips, thinning them out. She hardly glanced at Clara, who added peevishly, "It looked very good yesterday. It was a splendid piece of work when it was finished!" She looked at the surrounding nuns and followers, one by one. These sticklers, these narrow-minded, heartless, prim maids, old before their time. She glared at them with narrowed eyes and red cheeks as they gestured to each other with relish. Covering their prim little mouths to stifle their sniggers.

"No! I beseech you," Clara said, beginning to sound biblical in her efforts to reach what little sympathy lay at the bottom of their rigid hearts, "let us not laugh at the misfortunes...I mean...let's try to be kind...to one another...I'm sure if we were in the same position..." She trailed off and ran her tongue over the roof of her mouth. This gathering would never find themselves in the same embarrassing position. And she stood like a wilting flower, with her hands hanging limply at her sides. Her words became like boulders, too cumbersome to flow from her mouth. Her lips were too heavy to speak any more.

She wondered vaguely, as she watched the smirking faces around her, if this was a work of God—the paralyzing gloom spreading over her body and down into her soul. Maybe this was God having pity on her by clamping her mouth shut, silencing her. Through her dismal contemplation, she heard the indignant cry blown across the pond as a voice called out from the Saint Toole's side, "Did you *see* that? Did you *see?*" This was followed by a ripple of hostile protest, peppered with indignant jeers.

Clara felt herself jolted back into motion at the sight of the crowds surging forward from the other side of the pond. They floundered and broke into singles and scattered huddles as they reached its banks, dispersing confusedly as they all found different paths to reach their rival parade. The soldiers, having been more than content with shadowing the parades up to that point, hesitated ineffectively, glancing around uncertainly. Their inaction incited the milling crowds.

Participants and followers of the Saint Alba's pilgrimage jostled Clara as they split, surging forward to meet the enemy at the water's edge in combat, skirting around the banks to clash, hesitantly at first, then with growing malice and intention. Shouted insults were followed by fisticuffs, and head locks abounded around Clara. She felt a pang of bitter envy to see a knight on his steed ride up to and scoop up a maiden. Was that Burke, claiming his undying love for Ingrid? Clara even fancied they looked the part. Lucky Ingrid—men tumbling down from all corners to sweep her off her feet, while she, Clara, could not even have one mild-mannered tailor show her interest. Not for her the one man she longed for; she had only the cold silence of a cloister full of catty nuns to grow old with. The only men rushing toward her were obviously intent on battle with the men in her parade; they were certainly not looking for sweethearts. One or two men even plunged into the pond in their determined frenzy for battle. No, they lusted for combat rather than for love. One in particular was wading through the water with an eerie calm about his presence. She was not sure which was more spine chilling—his steady determination or his striking resemblance to Jack.

Chapter Twenty-One

For their part, as the Saint Toole's parade approached the duck pond, its leaders hesitated. Heading toward it from the other end were the Saint Alba's Jaw pilgrims, flanked by their supporters. They also seemed to flounder before heading round the bank to their left. At the same moment, the Saint Alba's pilgrim parade began moving round the pond from their right. Both teams stopped. The guards edged in to head them each round the edge of their side of the pond, so that they would pass one another from opposite sides of the water. With a peppering of mounted knights amongst the foot soldiers on the outskirts of both gatherings, and more soldiers eyeing them from the walls, it seemed certain that everyone would behave well.

As soon as Jack noticed the Saint Alba's pilgrims were filing toward and past the duck pond in the opposite direction, he began to lean first this way, then that, straining to catch a glimpse of Clara. He felt sure she'd be at the tail end, but he couldn't help looking out for her right from the head of the marchers.

"He's doing it again!" Ingrid said. "Burke. He has singled me out again."

Jack continued to peer across the pond. "Mm. That's fine."

"No it isn't!"

After waiting for Jack to respond for some time, Ingrid went on, "Mayhap he should be challenged." She paused again, to little effect. She stamped her foot. "Jack! Are you a man or a mouse? Make a stand!"

Yet still Jack would not turn his attention to Ingrid. He put his hands on her shoulders, steered her out of his way, and gazed beyond the pond.

"Challenge him!" Ingrid cried, glancing quickly behind her. "Now. Or you may lose your last chance..." But she may as well have tried to out moan the wind.

"Hark! I see her!" Jack grinned. "Aye, your words ring true!" For an instant, his grip tightened on her shoulders, and he kissed her cheek. "I thank you for your good advice. As you say, I shall seize the moment!"

Just then, the crowds and pilgrims on the other side of the pond slowed down dramatically as they stared across the wind-tousled waters, and someone gasped as a sniggering and pointing of fingers drifted across the aquatic barrier.

A shout bounded across the divide from the Saint Toole's parade, an angry shout, an indignant protest.

It was at this moment Jack broke from the crowd with long, bold strides. As he seemed intent on heading for the pond, the already charged citizens began to crackle with tightly sprung energy. Soldiers looked to the sheriff for his signal but they got none.

* * * *

Later, a spokesperson for the nuns of the Convent of Saint Alba's Jawbone said that the nun accused of causing the offence claimed she was merely gesturing to another nun, using innocent movements that successfully substituted for forbidden spoken words. But to the loud-voiced yokel across the pond who cried out with shocked indignation, the movement he saw was clearly a very rude gesture. A gesture indicating a smutty pun on the very name of Saint Toole. He later insisted that he was only telling the guards so that they could take the matter in hand. But in the seconds it took for both sides to boil over, the guards, waiting for orders from Burke, did nothing but stand dumbly by. The Saint Toole's crowd abandoned their heavenly choirs of praise, roared their indignation, and retaliated hotly with wagging jaw gestures. But as this was not half as smutty as Saint Alba's alleged gesture, their frustration grew rather than abated, and their plentiful laymen supporters surged forward toward the opposing side, as though they were following Jack.

Rather than retreating in a ladylike fashion, as one might have expected from the pilgrim marchers of Saint Alba's Jawbone, the youngsters of the crowd, followed quickly by an assortment of more respectable characters, surged forward to meet their attackers. And a brawl ensued. Some plunged right into the pond and began to wade across it, but most tussled on the muddy banks, slipping and sliding in the mud.

The soldiers failed to rush in and stop the fighting effectively, because Burke de Montfort did not give any clear signal to his men. He was too busy searching for Ingrid to see or hear the first ripples of the riotous wave. And when Jack broke out and ran into the duck pond, he drew Burke's attention not, as you might expect, to the start of the clash, but to the spot where Ingrid was. And seeing her standing with her arms folded, he spurred his horse to her. His soldiers could not interpret what this meant or what they should do about the fight breaking out under their noses, but they behaved admirably, if not under the guidance of God's Angels. They moved in, moved back out, wove in and out of the crowds and separated the individual little scuffles, before surrounding the reliquary bearers and the more serious members of each parade. Finally, they escorted them safely out of the heaving masses back onto the main road. The Saint Alba's pilgrims—including Clara's neighbor—were taken up to the Palmers' Guild church, and Father John, his curate and his assistant, and the choirboys hurried with their reliquary back to the old church on the poorer end of the main street.

Sheriff Burke de Montforte was spotted galloping off with a certain young woman seated in front of him on his horse. She offered little resistance when he swooped in and lifted her up onto his saddle, allowed him to kiss her roughly on the lips as they rode—indeed, she considered herself lucky that he didn't accidentally bite her tongue off—and she accepted his proposal as soon as she had wiped her mouth dry. Second best was better than nothing, she decided, as her first choice had just, as far as she knew, drowned himself in the duck pond, rather than take her hint.

* * * *

Jack was not, in fact, drowning in the duck pond. He had plunged himself into it without thinking of anything beyond keeping Clara in sight. Once the cold, murky water started to spread up to his knees, at which point he also registered how creepy the slimy bottom of the pond felt, with sharp, unidentifiable things poking at his soles through his sodden shoes, and unknown tendrils tentatively brushing past his calves, he realized the folly of his direct route. But as his thighs felt the first grip of chilliness, he was convinced Clara was standing stock still amidst the broiling crowds of insanely screeching, madly scurrying, and violently punching and kicking parties around her, and she was staring back at him, willing him across the pond toward her.

As the water crept up to his waistline, seeping into his calico undershirt, the question of the depth of the pond shot through his mind like a bolt from a crossbow. For another second he considered, almost rationally, doing the sensible thing and retreating to approach Clara by going around the pond. Pushing through the water with all his strength, he dismissed the idea for two reasons. Firstly, Clara seemed entranced, romantically, he hoped, in watching him going through such extremes to reach her. Humble tailor though he was, he was man enough to have no doubts that women adored this type of gesture. This was the sort of approach that could turn a lukewarm maybe to an arms-around-the-neck, tears-of-passion *yes*! And secondly, with men challenging each other randomly, attacking one another from behind, and fraying on the banks, going across the pond was the safest place to approach Clara without fear of interruption.

As the water's icy fingers gripped his chest, he told himself firmly he was not wading back, treading through that bed again, littered as it was with sordid debris. Clara, still standing, still locked in his gaze, was waiting on the other side. If he turned back then he'd have to lose sight of her—and, as she stood amongst the milling crowds, it could take too long; the moment could be lost by the time he found her again. *And enough of those precious moments had slipped past unused already.* Or, he could wade backwards through the pond. It was hard enough going, pushing his way forward. Apart from the fact that he'd look idiotic, if not altogether eerie, wading backwards while staring into her eyes. Clara would undoubtedly break eye contact and hurry away. Besides, he'd likely slip and fall, and be dragged to a watery death by the ghosts of previous drowning victims. And, as he adopted the mantra that he'd rather join them than live without Clara, he realized that the water was receding, down to his waist, then his thighs, and she was getting nearer. He could see her dark eyes, as forks of lightning flashed across the deepening gray of the sky. He could see her cheeks flush against her milky skin, wet with the first drops of rain. The gusts of wind were so strong, they tugged hard at her heavy skirts, showing the slender line of her long legs, as she held her short cape fast to her breast. And, yes, she *was* looking back at him!

Chapter Twenty-Two

Clara felt the burn of the wind in her eyes, but she refused to blink. How could she close her eyes and risk his not being there when she opened them? So many times that day she had believed she'd seen him, only to have her hopes dashed seconds later, when "he" turned out to be someone else, like that annoying jester. As the first icy drops of rain blown down from the clouds dropped on her face, she blinked at the shock of their cold touch. But he was still there. And he still looked exactly like Jack. She closed her eyes purposely, squeezing them shut. And when she opened them, he remained Jack. *Jack!* Her heart leapt at the thought of it really being him, coming toward her, getting closer.

He was more than looking her way; he was staring at her alone, she was sure. Dear God, let it be true, she prayed, and not just the crazed imaginings of a frustrated spinster, poised at the brink of... nunhood?

As she wondered if there was such a word, Clara became aware that her tightly clenched hand was crammed with a fistful of woolen cloth she clutched at her bosom. She hastily straightened her neckline and her skirts against the tugging wind, raised her hand to try and tidy her hair—but that was all securely tucked away in her wimple. Faltering, her hand dropped down to her sides as she stared dumbly at...yes. It was him. It was Jack, now emerging, dripping, from the shallows of the pond. His clothes were dark from being drenched, and they clung to him.

It was Jack and he was looking at her. She tried to gauge his expression, to fathom his mood, to guess his reason for seeking her out with such determination. She couldn't bear to deceive herself now. She'd never survive the crushing letdown if she assumed wrongly that he...

He was so close now. He was taking her hand in his hands. So strong, such elegantly long fingers folded over her fists, holding her in a tight grasp.

"Jack!"

"Don't," he breathed, "I beg of you, do not go, Clara."

"Not? But, Jack..."

He placed a finger on her lips, sending tingling sparks fizzing through her gloriously from head to toe and back again.

"Stay with me. I beseech you. Marry me. You shall never go hungry, Clara. I will always be good to you. I will live to please you."

"Oh." Clara sighed, as tears and rain blurred her vision. "Could I...? Dare I...? Disobey my father... I've begun to believe this is my obvious destiny, as I have remained so chaste all this time, despite my desires...I never wanted to, but...I've remained untouched, even while you were so close....and mayhap...'tis a sign from God that I'm destined to....not that I wish for that...I want, I yearn for you, I do...but..."

Jack shook his head slowly, his eyes blazing with such fiery determination that she felt a wave of fear.

"Nay, hush now, my sweet. My love." Then he pulled her to him. She felt his cold, wet clothes press against her as his lips closed over hers. Unashamed, his tongue found its way into her mouth, as his arms wrapped tightly around her body. They moved upwards until his hands clutched her shoulders, and he pulled away from her and said, "Marry me!"

"Yes, but...my father...my Lord..." she spluttered, a lump in her throat blocking her words. Her body trembled, her heart pounded as within and her soul cried out. How could she turn him away?

"I'm afraid..." she croaked.

He wiped a tear from her cheek. His hands cupped her face, and he let his fingers stray to the border of her wimple. Then, with a tug, he ripped it off and tossed it aside, caressing her hair as it tumbled onto her shoulders. And she gasped.

His lips fell again on her open mouth. Her tongue clasped his this time, making him groan. With one hand knotted in her hair, the other roaming down her neck to cup her breast, she felt her nipple harden beneath his caress. Her breathing deepened rapidly as he pressed her firmly to him.

Then he drew back, smiling to see how she fell towards him, her lips still slightly parted. They gazed at each other for a moment.

"There," he said huskily. "Now I have defiled you. You are not fit for a life of chastity any longer. Or shall I be bolder?"

"Yes! No! Yes...not here..." Clara said, unwittingly bearing her neck for him to ravage with kisses.

"Unhand that maid at once!" a shocked voice cried. "Defiling a novice-to-be! You'll be flayed for..."

"No!" Clara cried. "I'm his...we're going to be..."

An oversized soldier leaned his scarred face close to theirs and snarled, "If you're not married by dawn, I'll have you both in stocks!"

"Well, it seems we have no choice in the matter," Jack said briskly, taking Clara's hand in his.

"No...absolutely forced into it!" She grinned as, hand in hand, they raced across the green, playfully dodging the scattering crowds. They were followed by a host of friends, William, his father Howard, and the joiner.

As they ran down the main street, they spotted ahead of them the core of the Saint Toole's parade, scurrying with as much dignity as their haste would allow toward the church. The curate's assistant kept glancing behind him, and an agitated Father John cried out intermittently, "Steady on! Don't drop it!" Periodically, he reached out his hand in panic to catch the reliquary lest it fell, as it wobbled under the quick mincing of the curate and his assistant. The replica hand was noticeably absent.

Running faster, with Clara squealing as she almost tripped up on her long skirts, the two lovers caught up with the holy men. They begged Father John to marry them at once, but he shooed them away irritably. "Come back tomorrow before the morning Mass," he said.

"Father, that's almost a whole day away," Jack protested.

"What'll we do...what if...I mean not that we would, but what if..."

"Try to resist temptation until then, my dear child in God," the priest advised as he and his entourage swept up the steps and through the doors of Saint Toole's as they mysteriously opened from within. Clara and Jack stood at the bottom of the stairs and stared as the curate's assistant shut the doors behind them.

"Well, we'll do our best!" Jack called after them lamely.

"Yes, indeed...absolutely!"

"I'll tell you this much, I'm not letting you out of my sight until then!" And he slipped his arm round her waist, making her giggle as he whispered something in her ear.

* * * *

The next day, they stood exactly in the same spot, in very much the same embrace, and said their wedding vows, before being led into the church to celebrate Mass with William and their neighbors, and Howard the publican and his wife, etc., etc., all crowding round to support them. The sun, burning a thin veil of clouds away, lit up the contrast of the yellow belt with garnet studs against her velvet surcoat with new red and gold sleeves sewn onto it just the night before, by her new husband, with both abounding skill and love.

About the Author:

Fiona lives just outside London with her husband and three children.

She loves ancient history, mythology, folklore and especially all things Celtic. Her compassionate interest in people, her fascination with Britain's rich and colorful heritage, and her endearment to its picturesque land are reflected in her delightful storytelling. Fiona mostly writes fantasy and historical woman's fiction but also some children's fiction.

When she's not penning stories in a nook beneath the stairs, you may find her cooking up a storm in the kitchen, reading tarot cards, or just doing household chores. *Saint Alba's Jawbone*, a medieval tale, is her first story published by Eternal Press.

Her website can be found at
http://www.fionalaw.webs.com

Also from Eternal Press:

The Pendant
by Mirella Patzer

eBook ISBN: 9781770650466
Print ISBN: 9781770650510

Historical Romance
Novel of 92,000 words

A medieval tale of murder, desperation, and true love. A lost ancient treasure. A 100 year family feud. A woman with a passion richer than the bloodstone pendant she wears around her neck.

In medieval Italy, as spirited and stalwart as any man, the brazen Contessa Morena is betrothed to the impoverished, black-hearted Count Ernesto, a man desperate to escape his mounting gambling debts by marrying her and laying claim to the ancient treasure secreted somewhere in the underbelly of her castle.

Also from Eternal Press:

Carina And The Nobleman
by Jannine Corti Petska

eBook ISBN: 9781926640594
Print ISBN: 9781926647357

Romance Medieval
Novel of 78,000 words

Forced to the streets after her mother dies, Carina Gallo is desperate to survive and find her long lost sisters. Consumed with locating his missing brother, Count Luciano has forsaken his needs. When he catches beautiful and vulnerable Carina stealing from him, he takes pity and cares for her until she's strong enough to work off her crime. Carina is forever grateful to Luciano, yet fears he will learn of her wicked secret and condemn her to burn. Will Luciano and Carina find a way to feed the mutual passions they share, or will heresy and obsession with lost family destroy them both?

Breinigsville, PA USA
07 March 2011
257176BV00001B/29/P